TRIPPER & SAM

Danger on the Sound Track
Nancy K. Robinson

D1560614

AN
APPLE
PAPERBACK

SCHOLASTIC INC.
New York Toronto London Auckland Sydney

To my dear friend, Eva Moore,
editor *par excellence.* . . .

ISBN 0-590-33594-4

12 11 10 9 8 7 6 5 4 3 2 1   6 7 8 9/8 0 1/9

Printed in the U.S.A.   01

First Scholastic printing, November 1986

Other Apple Paperbacks
by Nancy K. Robinson:

Tripper & Sam #1
  The Phantom Film Crew

For younger readers:

Mom, You're Fired!
Oh Honestly, Angela!
Just Plain Cat
Wendy and the Bullies
Veronica the Show-Off

Special Acknowledgment

This book could not have been written without the expertise of Gene De Fever, David Eisendrath, and Richard Waddell.

PROLOGUE

Sam was Tripper's oldest friend. She had known him since she was a little girl. They had met one summer afternoon in Central Park.

It was a story they had both heard many times. . . .

Tripper's father, a documentary film director, had been shooting a film at the model boat lake. Every day a boy with reddish-gold curls showed up on his bicycle to watch the filming.

One afternoon Tripper arrived with her grandmother. She was clutching a small boat made of popsicle sticks.

"Whatever you do," her grandmother warned her, "don't fall in the lake."

Tripper took one look at her grandmother, ran to the deep end of the lake, and fell in.

Before anyone realized what had happened, the boy dropped his bicycle and ran to the spot where Tripper had disappeared. He lay down at the edge, reached in, and pulled Tripper out. He almost fell in himself.

Tripper lay on the ground soaking wet. Her eyes were closed. She wasn't moving. The boy began pressing his hand on her stomach. . .

". . . the way I've seen them do on those rescue shows on tv," he explained to a newspaper reporter later on. Water came out of Tripper's mouth.

"Are you breathing?" the boy asked her.

"No!" Tripper screamed and she began to cry.

The young hero was named Sam. Sam did not want a reward for saving Tripper's life. He just wanted to be allowed to hang around the film crew after school. He wanted to learn how movies were made. . . .

What Sound Doesn't Belong?

"When did you get back?" Sam asked Tripper. He stamped the snow off his heavy boots and sat down across from Tripper at the kitchen table.

"Last night," Tripper said. She was struggling to roll out cookie dough, but it kept sticking to the rolling pin. "I got in just in time for the blizzard. Isn't it exciting? Just think. A raging blizzard. The whole city of New York snowed in, and I finally get to spend my first Christmas at home. You know, I've never spent a Christmas at home."

Tripper went to boarding school in Colorado, but she usually spent her vacations with her father, Roger Tripper, and his film crew on location in different parts of the world.

Sam took the tape recorder he had hanging over his shoulder and placed it carefully on the table. He propped the long microphone he was carrying against the wall. Then he pulled down the hood of his polar expedition jacket, took off his headphones, and shook more snow out of his reddish-gold curls.

Ever since the day Sam fished Tripper out of the lake in Central Park, he had worked in her father's film office after school. Sam seemed to have an unusual talent for recording sound. During his vacations from high school, he went along with the film crew on location as assistant sound man.

Sam stretched out his long legs. "Well, I'm bored," he announced. "I wish we were going someplace. I'm in the mood for an adventure."

"Look, Sam," Tripper said. "I'm getting tired of adventures. Last year we didn't even *have* Christmas."

"It disappeared right off the map," Sam said.

The year before, Tripper and Sam had gone along with the film crew to New Zealand to film the last leg of a sailboat race. They had flown out of Los Angeles on Christmas Eve and arrived in New Zealand the next day. But it wasn't Christmas Day. It was December 26th. They had lost a whole day when they crossed the International Date Line on their way around the world.

Tripper's friends at school had been fascinated by that. "But where did Christmas *go*?" her best friend, Katy Bear, kept asking her.

"I don't know," Tripper told her. "That's what happens when you cross the date line going west. When you go east, you get two of the same day."

Sam watched Tripper as she tried to peel some sticky dough off the rolling pin.

Tripper sighed. "I just want to retire and bake cookies."

"Have you ever made cookies before?" he asked her.

"No," Tripper said. "It's a little harder than I thought it would be. Want to help?"

"Nope." Sam grinned at her. "I want *you* to help *me*."

"Do what?" Tripper asked.

"Test out a new windscreen for this rifle mike," Sam said.

Tripper looked at the long microphone propped up against the wall. She knew the rifle mike was designed to pick up sounds from very far away — not because it was more powerful, but because it didn't pick up all the other sounds around.

"I thought you didn't like to use the rifle mike," Tripper said.

"I don't," Sam said. "It tends to make things sound muddy, but sometimes I have to."

"Do we have to go outside to test the windscreen?" Tripper asked.

"Of course," Sam said. "That's where the wind is. Oh, come on, Tripper, I could use some help."

"But it's such a perfect evening to be *inside*," Tripper said. "Snowflakes pattering against the window. Wind howling around outside. Cozy warm kitchen. Batches of Christmas cookies about to be put in the oven. . . ."

Tripper gazed dreamily out the window. The kitchen was on the top floor of her father's townhouse. The rest of the townhouse was used as his film offices. It was on the corner of East 50th Street and Beekman Place on a bluff overlooking the East River.

Tripper looked sadly down at the cookie dough. "I don't get it. First it's too sticky.

Then I add flour, but it doesn't seem to want to hold together."

"Maybe the cookies will be ready by *next* Christmas," Sam suggested.

"Gee thanks, Sam," Tripper said.

"Is your Dad disappointed the wildlife film fell through?" Sam asked.

Tripper nodded. "Very disappointed. He really wanted to make a film about saving endangered species. The big convention starts next week in Costa Rica, but the International Wildlife Fund couldn't raise enough money in time to make the film. Dad's one hundred thousand dollars short of the budget he needs."

Sam sighed. "Boy, I'd do anything to get to Costa Rica."

"As a matter of fact," Tripper said, "a funny thing happened. We might get there after all. Do you know who Ted Barry is?"

"Sure," Sam said. "He owns one of the biggest travel agencies in the world. I've seen him on his tv commercials." Sam went on in a deep voice, " 'This is Ted Barry, president of Barry Tours, relaxing on this fun-filled cruise through the Himalayas. . . .' "

Tripper laughed. Sam did good imitations.

"Anyway," she went on, "Ted Barry moved into the house next door. He called Dad asking if Dad could do some travel films on Costa Rica. Dad's over there right now trying to talk him into putting the money into the wildlife film instead."

"You're kidding!" Sam said. "Why didn't you say something?"

Tripper shrugged. "I don't know. I guess I'm not all that interested in Costa Rica. I'm not particularly interested in any of those countries in Central America."

Sam stared at Tripper. "That really sounds dumb, Tripper," he said. "What's the matter with you?"

Sam noticed that Tripper's face was flushed. She was busy trying to cut out a star-shaped cookie from the sticky dough. She was working as if her life depended on it.

Suddenly Sam understood. Tripper's mother had been killed in Central America when Tripper was only three years old. Nell Tripper had been a photojournalist on assignment in Honduras when her car hit a land mine. Tripper's first name was Nell, too, but she never used it. "Just call me Tripper," she told anyone who asked.

Sam was quiet. He watched Tripper prying the sticky dough out of the cookie cutter. He stood up and took off his jacket.

He took a tape out of his bag and put it on the tape recorder.

"Now listen carefully, Tripper," he said. "What sound doesn't belong?"

He turned the knob and the tape began to play.

"Traffic noises," Tripper said. "Cars honking. Buses. That's all I hear. Traffic noises."

Sam wound the tape back. "Listen to it again," he said. "Listen carefully. What sound doesn't belong?"

"Is this a game?" Tripper asked.

"Sort of," Sam said. "It's a good way to train your ears to select out sounds."

He played the tape again.

Tripper shrugged. "I just hear traffic noises."

Sam handed her the headphones. "Try it with these," he said.

Tripper put on the headphones. She closed her eyes and listened. "Cars, trucks, buses. . . ." Suddenly she opened her eyes and grinned at Sam. "I hear a cow mooing. There's a cow mooing in the background."

"Right," Sam was pleased. "That sound doesn't belong."

"I get it," Tripper said.

"Now, listen to the next recording," Sam said.

Tripper put down her rolling pin and listened.

"An amusement park," she said. "I hear a carousel, shooting gallery, ice cream vendors. . . ."

The second time Sam played the tape through, she heard it.

"A typewriter!" she said. "I hear a typewriter. The typewriter doesn't belong!"

"Excellent!" Sam said. "Now the next one is hard."

Tripper closed her eyes and listened.

She heard waves rolling into a shore. Seabirds. More waves . . . and then a blood-curdling scream.

"Well, that was easy," Tripper said. "I would say the blood-curdling scream definitely does not belong."

"It certainly doesn't," Sam said.

Tripper looked at Sam. He was staring out the kitchen window. He had a funny look on his face.

"The blood-curdling scream wasn't on the tape," he said. "That was a real scream. And it came from right near by. Someone's in trouble!"

Tripper took off the headphones and ran to the kitchen window. She opened it and snow swirled in. All she could hear was the sweeping sound of wind and snow.

Then — for the second time — a terrible scream pierced the night.

Mac

Sam was on the kitchen phone calling the police.

Tripper was sure it was too late.

"Whoever that was must be dead by now," she said flatly. "Those were the worst screams I've ever heard."

Sam held up his hand for her to be quiet and gave the police the address. Then she heard him say, "Well, it *is* hard to tell where they're coming from. The sound bounces around a lot on this corner. But listen, I've got some sound equipment with me. If we hear the screams again, I think I'll be able to tell where they're coming from."

He listened for a moment. "Right," he said, "I'll meet you at the corner."

Sam pulled on his jacket and put the tape recorder on his shoulder. He put on his headphones and grabbed the long microphone.

"I'm meeting the police downstairs," he told Tripper. "They're getting a lot of calls on this, but everyone thinks the screams are coming from a different place."

"I'm coming, too!" Tripper said, but Sam was already on his way down the stairs.

Tripper ran to the hall closet and pulled on her rubber boots. She put on her long winter jacket and grabbed her camera bag. Her first thought was that she would get a picture of the murderer running away.

It was natural for Tripper to think that way. She was a photographer. She always took production stills of her father's film crew at work. She was a good photographer, but she only liked to photograph in black and white.

More shrieks. Tripper froze. She didn't feel so brave anymore. She wanted to turn back and hide.

But she couldn't let Sam face an escaping murderer all by himself.

Tripper ran down the stairs and into the street. She looked around for Sam. It was hard to see through the darkness and the falling snow.

Under the light of a lamppost she saw Sam, standing like a statue holding out the rifle mike. He adjusted his headphones and waited. Everything was quiet.

Tripper looked up. Many people in the surrounding buildings had their shades up and their curtains pulled back. They were staring down into the street.

Tripper started across the street and stepped into a deep snow drift. She felt the snow oozing into the top of her boots. Just at that moment the shrieks started up again. Tripper held her breath and watched Sam.

Sam turned slowly around in a circle holding the microphone out. He turned back halfway and held still.

Tripper scrambled out of the snow drift, clutching her camera under her jacket, and joined Sam under the lamppost.

"That's where the screams are coming from," Sam told her. "That's the loudest point."

Sam had the microphone pointed up toward the rooftop penthouse of the house next door to Tripper's. The penthouse was a modern concrete addition built onto the roof. It had a hothouse and terrace on one side.

Tripper's heart was pounding. Suddenly it seemed to stop dead still. Her head felt light.

Sam was pointing the microphone to Ted Barry's townhouse. Tripper started toward the house. *Her father was in there.*

Sam grabbed her and pulled her back. "Wait a minute, Tripper. Wait for the police."

"I will not," Tripper said. "Let me go. Dad's in there."

"They'll be here any minute," Sam said.

Tripper tried to pull away. "I'm not waiting for them. I know what I'll do. I'll just go up to our roof and cross over to theirs. They connect."

"No!" Sam said.

Just then two police cars pulled up. A policeman jumped out and came over to Sam. For a few seconds he just stared at Sam's sound equipment. Sam explained quickly. The policeman nodded and signaled to the other policemen.

"Wait here," he told Sam and Tripper. "We're going to check it out."

Tripper tried to follow the policemen across the street, but Sam pulled her back.

"Take it easy, Tripper," Sam said. "I'm sure your father's all right. Besides, those screams didn't really sound *human*."

Tripper felt a chill creep up her neck. "What do you mean by *that*?" she asked.

They watched as the policemen mounted the steps and rang the doorbell. A butler with sandy blond hair appeared. And a moment later Ted Barry came to the door.

They both recognized him from his tv commercials. Ted Barry looked more like an energetic Congressman than the owner of a large travel agency. He was wearing a dark gray pin-striped suit, a white shirt, and a red tie with polka dots. He had an even suntan and dark wavy hair graying at the temples.

He seemed irritated at having been disturbed. He listened impatiently. Then, all at once, he smiled and began to talk.

Tripper couldn't stand it another minute. "I'm going over there," she told Sam.

When Tripper got to the doorstep, Ted Barry was saying, "I can't tell you how sorry I am about this disturbance, officers. . . . Although, I suppose, when you think about it, it's all quite amusing. . . ."

Tripper squeezed in between two of the policemen. She was trembling with rage.

"I don't see what's so funny," she told Ted Barry. "And if you don't bring me my

father right now, I will call the police."

At that very moment there were four policemen standing around Tripper on the doorstep, but she didn't seem to notice.

Ted Barry's smile vanished. "What's this all about?" he asked abruptly.

Suddenly Sam was beside Tripper on the doorstep.

"She's Roger Tripper's daughter," he explained, "and what she's trying to say is . . . well . . . due to the commotion, she finds herself . . . um . . . a little concerned about her father's welfare."

Tripper had no time for diplomacy. "What have you done with him?" she demanded. Ted Barry's eyes were close together and so deep-set she couldn't see the expression in them. She was sure he was hiding something.

"Well, well — Roger Tripper's daughter. Rog didn't tell me he had such a good-looking daughter. He ought to put you in some of his films," Ted Barry said.

Tripper had been told that so many times she often forgot to say thank you. She just stood there staring at Ted Barry.

"My dear girl, there's nothing to worry about," Ted Barry said. "Rog and I are down in the screening room. I'm just show-

ing him one of our old travel films about Costa Rica."

He turned to the policemen. "You see, the screening room is completely sound-proof. That's why we didn't hear the racket coming from the penthouse. I *am* sorry Mac caused all this trouble."

The police seemed satisfied. One of them thanked Sam for his help. "That was good work," he said, and they left.

"Now, if you will excuse me." Ted Barry started to close the door.

Tripper was still confused. "Wait a minute," she said. She found herself staring at Ted Barry and wondering if he used a blow-dryer on his perfectly waved hair.

"Let's go, Tripper," Sam whispered. "We're interrupting a business meeting."

But Tripper didn't budge.

"Your father is safe and sound," Ted Barry assured her. "Would you like me to tell him you're here?"

Suddenly Tripper was embarrassed. She knew how important the wildlife film was to her father. She shook her head.

"Another time I'll invite you up to the penthouse to meet my son," Ted Barry said. "He's just turned eleven, but I'm afraid he's been a little out of sorts lately. De-

pressed, if you know what I mean."

"Is that why he has these little . . . um
. . . bursts of temper?" Tripper asked as
politely as she could.

"Who?" Ted Barry asked.

"Your son," Tripper said. "Mac."

Mr. Barry seemed to find that very
amusing. He looked at his watch. "Well,
I guess I have a few minutes before the
film's over. Come along."

He led them to a wide marble staircase.
"I'll introduce you to Mac. I think you're in
for a big surprise."

Windows facing onto a terrace lined one
wall of the penthouse apartment. On another wall there was a large bookcase filled
with comic books. Mac was in a cage hanging from the bookcase. He was chained to
a perch.

"A parrot made that noise?" Tripper
asked. She stared at Mac. She had never
seen such a large parrot with such brilliant colors. He was scarlet with iridescent
blue and gold wings. He stood out from the
bookcase like a large jewel.

"He's a scarlet macaw!" Sam said.
"They're amazing!"

"Oh, Mac is worth a fortune," Ted Barry

said. "A bird like this is an excellent investment."

"Investment?" Sam was standing in front of the cage watching Mac. Mac cocked his head to one side and blinked at Sam.

"Hello, Mac," Sam said.

Mac tucked his head down and ruffled his brilliant red, blue, and gold feathers.

"An excellent investment," Ted Barry went on. "In fact, we just found a woman willing to pay us three thousand dollars for Mac. She's going to redecorate her entire living room to match his feathers. We probably could have gotten more, but, naturally, our first concern is that Mac have a good home."

"Aren't there restrictions about bringing scarlet macaws into the country?" Sam asked.

"Indeed there are," Ted Barry said, "and very important ones they are for the protection of our feathered friends in the wild. I am happy to say that Mac was born and bred in captivity. Naturally we have the papers to prove it."

Ted Barry turned to Tripper. "I can see your friend really appreciates a bird like this. Unfortunately little Theo here is totally unable to relate to Mac."

"Dumb bird," said a voice from some-place.

Tripper looked around for the voice.

"Theo!" Mr. Barry said sharply. "Stand up and say hello to your guests." He seemed to be addressing a large pile of horror comic books spread out on a leather and chrome couch. Two feet wearing black Oxford shoes stuck out from the middle of the pile.

Mr. Barry turned back to Sam. "Interested in macaws?" he asked.

"Not in cages," Sam said quietly. "Not a bird like this."

When Sam turned to face Mr. Barry, Tripper got a shock. Sam's green eyes had a pained look in them. His wide thin mouth that was always slightly turned up at the corners was turned up even more.

But Tripper knew Sam wasn't smiling. He was very upset. Sam loved animals more than anyone Tripper knew.

"Now, now," Mr. Barry said. "We seem to have a slight philosophical difference here. These scarlet macaws make excellent pets."

"They bite," said the dull voice from the pile of comic books, "chew up furniture, and scream. This one is so dumb it won't even roller-skate."

"Roller-skate?" Tripper found herself talking to the pile of comic books, too. "Why would a parrot want to roller-skate?"

A boy's head emerged from behind a comic book. Ted Barry's son had not inherited his father's looks.

Theo had pale bulgy eyes, thick pouty lips, and almost no chin. He was wearing a pin-striped suit, just like his father's, but it was all rumpled. He rubbed his nose hard and looked blankly at Tripper.

"What good is a parrot that won't do tricks?" he asked. "This one won't even talk."

"Some birds won't talk," Sam said. "They have their own language in the jungle."

Ted Barry winked at Tripper. "Sounds like we have some kind of an expert here."

"I've read a lot about parrots," Sam said.

"I could have taught him to talk," Theo whined, "but Dad wouldn't let me. This kid Harold told me how to do it."

Ted Barry suddenly seemed to be in a big hurry. "Well, well, isn't it nice that you young people got a chance to meet. . . ."

Sam ignored Mr. Barry. "How were you planning to teach Mac to talk?" Sam asked Theo. "What did this kid Harold tell you to do?"

"Well." Theo glanced at his father and smirked. "All you have to do is slit their tongues a little. . . ."

Tripper felt sick.

". . . you see, it makes the tongue more agile," Theo went on.

"That's a lie," Sam said. "The bird will die."

"What do you know?" Theo muttered. "Besides, Dad didn't even give me a chance to try it."

"That's enough," Ted Barry said in a cold, quiet voice.

Theo glared at his father. Then he shrugged and picked up a comic book. "There's only one way to find out," he said.

Ted Barry didn't seem to hear that remark. He was looking at his watch. "Now," he said, "if you two will be kind enough to excuse me. . . ."

Before Tripper and Sam knew what was happening, they were being rushed down the stairs. The butler appeared with their jackets and showed them out the door.

Rooftop Mission

Roger Tripper leaned back in the plush velvet armchair in Ted Barry's screening room and watched the last few minutes of *Costa Rica: Land of Paradise*. It was the worst travel film he had ever seen.

He was sure he was wasting his time. Why would Barry Tours put money into a wildlife film that was purely educational? There would be no sales pitch for the travel agency.

A young man named Alonso was helping himself to a lavish spread of cold cuts, cheeses, and pickles laid out on the large conference table. Alonso was supposed to be working the projector.

Roger thought about Tripper and how much he had missed her in the last few months. He wished he were at home eating her homemade Christmas cookies. He could almost smell them baking.

The film was over. Alonso had to dash back to the projector to turn it off.

Just as the lights came up, Ted Barry walked back into the screening room.

"Well, what did you think?" he asked Tripper's father.

"Quite honestly," Roger said dryly, "I thought it was pretty terrible."

To his surprise Ted laughed and said, "I couldn't agree with you more."

"Besides," Roger went on, "I don't think we can have anything to do with an organization that promotes the hunting and killing of rare animals."

"Hold on a minute," Ted said. "You have to understand that that film was made when my father was still running Barry Tours. My father and I never saw eye to eye on these hunting expeditions. In fact, ever since he retired, I've put quite a lot of our profits into a small foundation dedicated to the preservation of wildlife."

Roger looked at Ted Barry. Maybe there *was* a chance. Maybe they could get the rest of the money for the film in time. The convention on endangered species started next week. In any case, Ted Barry was his last hope.

Tripper was worried about Sam. He hadn't said a word since they got back to the kitchen. She scraped pieces of the cookie dough together and tried to form them into a lump. She had lost all interest in baking.

Suddenly Sam said, "Do you think he might do it?"

"Do what?" Tripper asked.

"Slit Mac's tongue," Sam said.

Tripper thought a moment. "Well, to tell you the truth," she said, "I think Theo was just saying that to annoy his father. It must be hard to have a father who's that 'perfect.' "

"Did you notice that Mac was missing a toe?" Sam asked.

"No!" Tripper stared at him. "Why would he be missing a toe?"

"I don't know," Sam said miserably.

Tripper decided to change the subject. "How's Binker?" she asked. Tripper wasn't particularly interested in Sam's dog. She didn't care much for Binker, a black lump of a dog who always seemed to be daydreaming about something.

Sam perked up. "You know, an interesting thing happened," he said. "We put Binker into dog obedience school this fall."

"Oh yeah?" Tripper tried to sound interested.

"It was amazing," Sam said. "He got expelled."

"What?" Tripper turned to look at Sam. "Binker got kicked out of dog obedience school?"

"Yup," Sam said. "He kept falling asleep."

Tripper wasn't surprised.

"Mom and I figured it out," Sam went on. "You see, Binker is much too intelligent to fall for that kind of stuff. He has too much imagination to go for that approval nonsense — the little pats on the head . . . 'Good doggie,' and all that."

Tripper tried not to smile. She was considering just throwing all the cookie dough away. Instead she stuck it into the refrigerator to get it out of the way.

"We've got to do something," Sam burst out. He went to the window and stared out into the darkness. He turned around and looked steadily at Tripper for a few seconds.

"Does your roof really connect to their terrace?" he asked.

Tripper stared at Sam. "You're not thinking about *rescuing* Mac, are you?"

"Of course not," Sam said. "We would just be checking on him."

Things were going much better than Roger Tripper had expected. Ted Barry did not seem surprised at the amount of money needed to complete the budget ". . . so long as you keep within that ball park figure," he told Tripper's father.

Roger took the film proposal out of his briefcase. "Our plan is to have the film crew cover the wildlife convention in San José. At the same time we will be sending a second unit — a smaller film crew — into the jungle on the Osa Peninsula at Corcovado Reserve."

"Corcovado?" Ted Barry sat up straight. "Excellent choice!" he said. "The last virgin rain forest left in all Central America. Alonso, did you hear that?"

Alonso was back at the table helping himself to more food. He had sharp features and straight dark hair. He was wearing a white satin jogging outfit.

"Alonso does research for our foundation," Ted explained. "He's a graduate student in ecology down at the University of San José. A fine researcher if I may say so."

At that moment Alonso was researching the different types of olives on a plate of cheeses. He turned around and said with a heavy Spanish accent, "You will be interested to know there are one hundred thirty-nine species of mammals on the Corcovado Reserve, not to mention one hundred sixteen species of amphibians and reptiles, including the American crocodile. In addition, one will be able to find three hundred species of birds, with Corcovado having the largest population of scarlet macaws. . . ."

"Yes, yes, yes." Ted Barry cut him off. "Hold on a minute, Rog. You can't film there. Only scientists can get onto that reserve. It's run by the National Park Service of Costa Rica."

"We've already gotten permission from them to film there," Roger Tripper said quietly.

"You don't say!" Ted was silent. Then he suddenly seemed to make up his mind.

"Well, well," he said. "It looks like it's all systems go. I can't tell you how honored I am to be able to assist you in such a worthwhile project." He paused and said, "However, there is one condition. . . ."

"What's that?" Roger asked.

". . . that Barry Tours be allowed to make all travel arrangements within Costa Rica. We have our own light aircraft and can transport your crew to the jungle station. We would also want to provide the guide for the crew. Alonso here is an excellent guide and translator."

Roger Tripper didn't think that sounded too bad. "Just as long as no one interferes with the film crew or the content of the film," he said.

Ted Barry agreed to that.

A phone buzzed on a desk in the corner.

"Excuse me," Ted said and he went to pick up the phone.

He listened. Suddenly he became tense. He turned and signaled to Alonso. "Alonso," he said, "someone's set off the silent burglar alarm on the terrace. Go up and find out what's going on."

Alonso put his sandwich down. "No problem," he said and he left the screening room.

"Shouldn't you call the police?" Roger asked.

"Oh, I don't think that will be necessary at this point in time," Ted Barry said. "Alonso is perfectly capable of handling the situation. You have to understand that Alonso is also a student of the martial arts — a black belt in karate."

He settled himself into one of the velvet armchairs, stretched out his arms, and began massaging the back of his neck.

"Believe me, Rog," he said. "Everything is under control."

The wind was blowing from the northeast. It made an eerie sound as it whipped around the skylight on the roof of Tripper's townhouse.

It was still snowing hard, but the snow hadn't accumulated much on the roof. The concrete structure on Ted Barry's townhouse had acted as a windbreak. Tripper and Sam had little trouble getting across the roof.

Tripper followed the light from Sam's flashlight to the edge of the terrace next door. Sam climbed over the parapet and held the flashlight for Tripper. Then he switched it off.

"Stay out of the lighted areas," he whispered.

There was a large patch of light that stretched across the snow — the light from Theo's penthouse apartment. It was only dark along one edge of the terrace where drapes covered a row of windows.

They crept along in the darkness and hid behind the drapes. There was no danger of their being heard. The television inside was blasting with the shrill sound track of a horror movie.

Tripper and Sam peeked around the edge of the drapes into Theo's apartment.

Theo was sitting on the edge of the couch, his eyes glued to the television set. Mac was in his cage. Every once in a while he blinked at the television set.

Sam pulled Tripper close and whispered, "Now can you see that Mac's missing a toe? Look at his right foot."

Theo suddenly got to his feet and, with his eyes still glued to the set, he picked up a blanket that was lying on the arm of the couch. He backed away in the direction of Mac's cage.

Sam started forward, but Tripper pulled him back. "Wait," she whispered.

Theo was covering Mac's cage with the blanket. To their surprise, he even took his eyes away from the horror movie to make sure the entire cage was properly covered.

Sam sighed with relief. "That's what he's supposed to do," he whispered. "You're supposed to keep a parrot out of the draft at night."

"I told you he was only saying those things to annoy his father," Tripper said.

A loud car commercial came on the tv. Theo's eyes wandered over to the windows and he stared out at the snow. He rubbed his nose.

Tripper and Sam ducked back.

"Let's go," Sam whispered. "I guess it's all right."

Tripper turned around and started back.

"Tripper!" Sam whispered. "I *told* you to stay out of the light!"

"I'm not *in* the light," Tripper said crossly. "You're the one casting that shadow."

But it didn't make sense. Sam was directly behind her in the dark area, and the only source of light was those windows.

Suddenly the shadow moved. There was a loud guttural yell, and Tripper looked around in time to see Sam receive a flying kick to the head.

Shadows in the Cutting Room

Sam lay on the ground. Snowflakes bounced lightly off his cheeks. He was out cold.

"Say something," Tripper begged him. "Please say something, Sam."

She looked up at the dark-haired young man who was jogging in place to keep warm.

"Now look what you've done!" she said angrily.

The young man stopped jogging and stared at Tripper.

Just then Sam groaned. He sat up and rubbed his eyes with his heavy woolen gloves. He looked up at Tripper and then at the young man who was watching them both like a hawk.

"What did you do that for?" Sam asked him.

"You are not robbers?" Alonso asked in surprise.

"No, we are not robbers," Tripper said coldly, "and many people consider it extremely bad taste to kick people first and ask questions later."

Alonso looked down at his feet and began to fidget. "But I only do what — "

"Good work, Alonso!" Ted Barry was crossing the terrace in long strides. He had put a heavy sheepskin jacket on over his suit and was wearing a red and black checked hunting cap with earflaps. He stopped short when he recognized the trespassers.

Sam got to his feet and brushed off the snow. "We were just checking on Mac," he explained.

"I see," Ted said in an even voice. "And are you satisfied?"

Tripper and Sam looked at each other.

"Perhaps we should all have a little pow-wow," Ted Barry said and he led them inside.

As it turned out Ted was very understanding about the whole incident.

"Naturally you were concerned," he said, "but, in the future, please come to

me with any little problems or questions
you might have."

Tripper's father was *not* so understanding.

"Don't ever do anything like that again,"
he told Tripper and Sam on the way home.
"First of all, it's dangerous; secondly, it's
illegal — and, I might add, it's not terribly
good for business."

Tripper and Sam trudged alongside him
in the snow without saying a word. They
knew they had almost ruined his chances
of making the wildlife film.

Roger Tripper came to a halt in front of
their townhouse.

"Tripper," he said crossly, "did you leave
the light on in the cutting room?"

Tripper shook her head and looked up
at the window. Shadows were moving back
and forth behind the blinds.

"Now what?" her father sounded very
tired.

Tripper felt discouraged. There would
be more police — more excitement.

"What a nice cozy evening we're having," she muttered to Sam.

"But who could be in there?" Sam asked.

"Elves, of course," said a voice behind them.

The three of them turned around and saw Coco. Coco was the electrician on Roger Tripper's film crew. Her eyes sparkled and her cheeks were pink from the cold. She was loaded down with shopping bags.

"Welcome home," she said to Tripper. "And welcome to our first Christmas party!"

In the corner of the cutting room was a tree that reached all the way up to the ceiling.

"It's beautiful!" Tripper said to John.

John shrugged. "I just happened to pass a tree farm on my way in from the country. It fit in the van so...."

John was the grip on the film crew. He did all the carpentry that was needed to be done on the set. John was very shy.

"I've never had a Christmas tree before," Tripper said.

John nodded, but he refused to look at Tripper. He mumbled something about the tree not being straight and went to adjust the stand.

Tripper was surrounded by familiar faces. The entire film crew was there. Her father had worked with the same crew since she was little.

Eva, the film editor, was sitting on her editing stool. She was wearing the blue jeans and cable-knit sweater she always wore, and her straight blonde hair swung back and forth as she worked. But she wasn't editing film. She was cutting Christmas tree ornaments out of scraps of colored gels that were usually used as filters for the big movie lights.

Nick, the cameraman, was wearing a comfortable plaid wool shirt. He winked at Tripper as he poured out a cup of hot mulled cider for Leroy, her father's unit manager.

Tripper saw her father smiling at her. She found herself thinking that her father had chosen a very nice family for her.

Coco was busy dumping out the shopping bags under the tree. They were filled with Christmas presents.

"Who are all those presents for?" Tripper asked.

"Everyone," Coco said. "Presents for everyone. I've been shopping all day."

Coco loved to shop. She found shopping very interesting.

"But there are no names on the presents," Sam said.

"Of course not," Coco said. "You see, the trick of shopping for presents is never to have anyone in mind. If you try to figure out what people *want*, it spoils everything. . . ."

"It does?" Tripper asked.

"Yes," Coco went on. "When I shop for presents, I go into this special trance. And despite what people say, it is not the thought that counts. . . ."

"It's not?" Sam asked.

"No," Coco said. "It's the *surprise* that counts." She looked around at the beautifully wrapped presents under the tree. She sighed happily. "I wonder what *I* got."

"We have another surprise," Tripper's father announced.

"What's that?" Tripper asked. "Oh, yes, we're making the wildlife film!"

"No," her father said. His eyes twinkled. "Your homemade Christmas cookies! I've been dreaming about those cookies all evening!"

Second Unit

It was the day after New Year's and Tripper was still handing out homemade Christmas cookies. Everyone on the plane to Costa Rica enjoyed them very much.

"*Graçias, senorita. Delicioso.*" The passengers thanked her in Spanish and in English.

"We made too many," Tripper explained to the stewardess, who seemed especially fond of the gingerbread men. "The trick is getting the dough cold, and, by mistake, I had put the dough in the refrigerator. Dad said that was the right thing to do."

They were standing in the aisle. Roger Tripper and the film crew were sitting toward the back of the plane. Everyone else seemed to be talking and laughing.

"This flight seems like one big party,"

Tripper said. "Is it always this friendly?"

"Always." The stewardess smiled. "Costa Rica is a small country and a very friendly one."

On the way back to her seat Tripper passed Coco, who was reading a fashion magazine. Carlos, the assistant cameraman, was sitting next to her. He was busy checking out a box of camera attachments.

She had to climb over Gene, the chief soundman, to get to her seat. Gene was fast asleep and covered from head to toe with a blanket. She sat down next to Sam. Sam was reading a wildlife magazine.

"Tripper, did you know the jaguar is the third largest cat in the world? The lion, the tiger, and then the jaguar."

"Are there jaguars in Costa Rica?" Tripper asked.

Sam nodded. "Yes, but in Costa Rica, they're called *el tigre* — the tiger." He turned the page and kept reading.

Tripper's father was in the row of seats behind them. He was discussing the script with Nick, the cameraman, and Leroy, the unit manager.

Nick was grumbling. "Talking heads," he complained. "The whole film is going to be talking heads. Just a bunch of scientists blabbing, with some animal shots cut in. It'll be all talk."

"I know." Tripper's father sounded depressed. "I wish we had had more time to develop a story line — you know, something to tie the film together."

Tripper sighed and began reading the jaguar article over Sam's shoulder. There was a picture of Dr. Maria Vasquez, the woman who had written it.

"She's delivering the first paper at the convention," Sam told Tripper. "We'll probably meet her."

Tripper looked more closely at the picture.

"Sam," Tripper said suddenly. "I just gave her a cookie.

"Dad!" Tripper turned around. "I just gave Dr. Maria Vasquez a cookie. She's sitting right up there!"

In no time at all, Roger Tripper was standing in the aisle deep in conversation with Dr. Maria Vasquez, a pretty young woman with short curly dark hair and a wonderful slow smile. Tripper had introduced her father as a documentary film director "and the brains behind the cookies."

Sam was still reading, but now he was

reading a newspaper called the *Tico Times*. It was an English-language newspaper published in Costa Rica. He was reading an article on parrot smuggling and the diseases parrots can carry, such as Newcastle's virus which can wipe out another country's poultry industry.

"I don't get it," he said. "Why would anyone even *want* a parrot for a pet?"

"Well," Tripper began, "I know how you feel about it, but I can sort of see how — "

"Do you realize that, for every parrot that makes it to the pet store, at least ten have died along the way? Tripper, I'm talking about *legally* imported birds. Thousands more die in the illegal trade. Smugglers stuff them into tiny crates, hairdryers, even into the hub caps of cars. . . ."

Tripper was shocked.

Just then her father came down the aisle. He was very excited. "Leroy!" he called. "We got our story. It's all set. Right after Dr. Vasquez delivers her paper tomorrow morning, she'll fly out to the jungle with the film crew. She's been studying the jaguars on the Corcovado Reserve for years. She's delighted at the chance to continue her studies. The second unit will film her at work!"

"Sounds great!" Leroy said. "I just hope there's room on the plane. I talked to Ted Barry last night about the travel arrangements. He said the plane was a six-seater, but you forgot to tell me he was planning to go along with the film crew."

"What?" Tripper's father asked. "Is that what he told you?"

"Yes," Leroy said. "I have to admit I was sort of surprised."

"Well, it's news to me," Roger said. "I hope he doesn't think he's getting a free commercial out of this."

Leroy began in a deep voice: " 'This is Ted Barry, president of Barry Tours, relaxing among the crocodiles of Central America. . . .' "

Leroy did pretty good imitations, too.

"Barry is supposed to meet us at the airport," Roger said. "We'll discusss it then."

"We should decide on our second unit film crew right now," Leroy said.

"Well," Roger began, "we'll send Carlos — Nick can shoot the convention without an assistant. And, let me see . . . Sam can handle the sound."

Sam sat up straight in his seat. "I don't believe it!" he said. "I'm going to the jungle!"

"We'll need one more person to help out," Leroy said.

"What about Coco?" Tripper's father asked.

Tripper looked over at Coco, but she never looked up from her fashion magazine.

"We can't spare Coco," Leroy said. "The hotel is forty-five minutes outside San José — in the mountains. There may be electrical problems."

Roger Tripper was quiet. Good lighting was very important to him.

"Send Tripper!" Sam called over his shoulder.

Tripper thought Sam was joking. Then she heard Leroy say, "That's not a bad idea. She certainly knows her photography. She'd make a good assistant to Carlos."

Tripper held her breath.

"It's funny," her father said slowly. "Dr. Vasquez was just saying how much Tripper would enjoy it there. The jungle station at Sirena is supposed to be fairly comfortable from what I understand. There are beds, but they will have to bring mosquito netting and sheets, too."

"Well," Leroy said, "we'll have to shop for the supplies as soon as we get in. I'll take the three of them right from the air-port into San José."

There was a crackling over the loud-speaker of the airplane.

"Attention, passengers. If you look over to your right, you'll be able to see the coast of Central America. The dark line of forest marks the border between Honduras and Nicaragua. . . ."

All at once Tripper felt her throat tighten. Somewhere below her was the spot where her mother had been killed — where her mother's car had hit a land mine al-most ten years ago. She felt dizzy.

There was a hand on her shoulder. She looked up.

"Sometimes it helps to look," her father said gently. "I always do."

Sam pulled back so Tripper could see past him out the window. She looked down at the sparkling waters of the Caribbean and the coast line. She watched the dark line of forest fade into the distance. It seemed far away and very beautiful. She sat back in her seat.

"You okay?" Sam asked.

Tripper nodded. For some reason she suddenly felt light and free.

When their plane touched down at the airport outside San José, everyone clapped and cheered the pilot.

Tripper was amazed.

"Do they always do that?" she asked.

Sam was grinning at Tripper. "Maybe they're clapping for you, too," he said.

It was the beginning of summer in Costa Rica. As they waited on line to go through customs at the airport, Sam read the rest of the article on parrot smuggling. When their turn came, Sam absentmindedly put his bag and sound equipment on the counter in front of the customs inspector and turned to Tripper.

"That's it!" he said. "I knew it didn't make sense."

"What are you talking about, Sam?" Tripper asked. She put her leather overnight bag on the counter and smiled at the customs inspector.

"Didn't Ted Barry say Mac was born and bred in captivity?"

"Yes," Tripper said. "He said he had the papers to prove it."

"But don't you see," Sam said, "a bird born and bred in captivity wouldn't be missing a toe. It says here that they lose toes when they're transported illegally in crowded conditions. Someone gave Ted Barry a set of phony papers. Mac's a *laundered* bird!"

"Well, it's too late, anyway," Tripper said. "He already sold Mac to that woman."

"But do you know what *that* means?" Sam asked. "That means, whether he knows it or not, Ted Barry is trafficking in illegal goods!"

Tripper noticed that the customs inspector was looking at Sam. She wondered how much English he understood.

"Um . . . Sam . . ." Tripper said. "I wonder if this is the best place to discuss this particular subject."

"But I've got to show this article to Ted Barry," Sam said. "I've got to show it to him right away."

"That should be easy," Tripper said. "He's standing right behind you."

Ted Barry was dressed in a short-sleeved mustard-colored safari outfit. He looked like an advertisement for *Hunting World.* He glanced at Sam as if he had never seen him before and said to Tripper, "Well, well, your father didn't tell me you were bringing a friend."

"A friend?" Tripper asked. "What do you mean. Sam is a member of the film crew."

"Is that so?" Ted Barry turned abruptly and called, "Rog — may I have a word with you?"

Just then Carlos came hurrying over.

"Let's go," he said to Tripper and Sam. "Leroy has a taxi waiting outside to take us into San José. We've got to shop for supplies."

Coco was standing nearby. "Are you going shopping without me?" she asked sadly. "What are you shopping for?"

Carlos laughed. "Mosquito netting, insect repellent, maps, heavy cotton socks. . . ."

"Now be sure you find out where the cotton in the socks has been grown," Coco advised.

As they were leaving the waiting room, Tripper overheard her father say sharply to Ted Barry, "Despite his age, Sam happens to be one of the best soundmen in the business, and I will not stand for a sponsor interfering in any way with this production. . . ."

Carlos whisked them out the door.

Shopping
for the Jungle

"But of course you speak Spanish, Carlos," Tripper said somewhat desperately.

The assistant cameraman shook his head. "A lot of people think I do just because my name is Carlos," he said. "I guess Leroy thought so, too. I was born in New York City. My parents came from Puerto Rico, but they always spoke English at home. I thought you two spoke Spanish."

Carlos, Tripper, and Sam were standing on a busy street corner in San José, the capital city of Costa Rica. Leroy had dropped them off and had gone on to make final arrangements with the National Park Service.

Traffic moved fast in San José. The sidewalks were crowded with people. The sun was hot. There was quite a lot of wind in

San José. Tripper felt chilly in her light blue cotton sun dress. To make matters worse, her dress kept blowing up around her.

Tripper always wore old-fashioned cotton bloomers under her dresses. She found the bloomers practical when she was climbing around taking photographs, but now she was getting quite a lot of stares from people passing by. It was making her cross.

"The second unit is sure off to a great start," Sam muttered.

Tripper turned on Sam. "Well, sarcasm isn't going to help."

They were standing in front of a camping store. It was closed.

"I don't understand," Carlos said. "Leroy said all shops here close between noon and two for lunch, but it's almost two-thirty."

Just then they saw a familiar figure jogging toward them. Alonso was dressed in tennis whites.

"I am here," he announced.

"Just in time," Carlos said. "Can you tell us why this store is still closed?"

"Tico time," Alonso said.

"What is 'Tico time'?" Carlos asked.

"Well," Alonso began, "we Costa Ricans call ourselves Ticos and here in San José we say that the stores open *exactly* between two and three."

Carlos laughed. "But that doesn't make sense."

"Oh, but it does," Alonso said earnestly. "You see, if you say that a store will open at two o'clock and that store does *not* open at two o'clock, then people they will be disappointed and there is a problem. But if you say it will open exactly between two and three, there is no problem."

Carlos smiled. "I guess time works differently in the tropics. Well, maybe you can help us with our list of supplies. None of us seems to speak Spanish."

"No problem," Alonso said.

"No problem" seemed to be Alonso's favorite expression. In no time at all they had finished most of the shopping, except for Tripper's boots . . .

". . . which I don't need, anyway," Tripper said. "I'll just wear my leather Italian sneakers. Besides, this is the only day we have to see San José."

They were sitting on a bench in a small park, which was filled with beautiful trees and flowers. There was a bandstand in the middle. A group of school children on holiday were standing in line in front of them watching them with friendly interest.

"You need boots," Sam insisted. "You don't understand. We're going into the jungle."

"Tropical rain forest," Alonso corrected him. He was following their discussion the way he might follow a tennis match. "You see, the scientific name for that area is actually 'tropical rain forest' — "

Sam cut him off. "This is serious, Tripper. I've read a lot about it. There are poisonous plants, snakes. . . ."

Tripper turned to Alonso. "Have you been to the Osa Peninsula?"

"Oh yes," Alonso said. "Many times. I know that area — how do you say — like the back of my hand."

"Well, then, tell him I don't need boots."

Alonso looked helplessly from Tripper to Sam.

"Don't drag him into it," Sam said. He turned to Carlos. "Tell Tripper she needs boots."

Tripper gasped. "That's not fair!"

"It probably *is* a good idea," Carlos said. "Sam and I both have boots. Ticks are a big problem and you should probably tape your pants inside your boots. It's very important to protect your feet and legs. An open cut or bite in the jungle — "

"Tropical rain forest," Alonso seemed very concerned with scientific accuracy.

"Anyway," Carlos went on, "in that kind of humidity, an open wound will fester. It can easily become infected and then you're in trouble!"

"Ha!" Sam said triumphantly.

Tripper was furious. "You can't vote on *my* feet. This is not a national election."

Alonso roared with laughter. He seemed to find Tripper's remark very funny. It only made Sam angrier. "Tripper," he said coldly, "if you don't do what we say, I'm going to tell your father I'm sorry I suggested you go with us."

Tripper was horrified. Sam was treating her like a child.

He was even worse in the shoe store. It was a tiny store. Boots and shoes were lined up along the rafters near the ceiling. The salesman spoke English. He had even lived in New York City for a while.

Tripper looked over the boots, but before she could pick a pair Sam said, "Those."

And he pointed to the ugliest boots Tripper had ever seen.

"They have square toes," Tripper said.

"She'll try them on," Sam told the salesman.

"They're fine," Tripper mumbled before she had even laced them halfway up. She wasn't planning to wear them, anyway.

"The right foot looks too big," Sam told the salesman.

Tripper felt humiliated, but she tried on a smaller size. She was about to take them off when Sam said to the salesman, "You don't have to pack them; she'll wear them now. She has to break them in."

Tripper's face was bright red.

They now had plenty of time before they had to meet Leroy. Alonso seemed to enjoy showing them San José. He loved explaining things: "This is our National Theater. You will be interested to know that it is modeled after the Paris Opera House." He was full of facts.

Tripper hadn't said a word to Sam since they left the boot store.

"Still mad about the boots?" Sam asked her.

Tripper didn't answer. She didn't want

to tell Sam that they were the most comfortable boots she had ever worn in her life. They were made of very soft leather. She felt as if she were walking on air.

After a while, she said, "It's not the boots; it's the way you treated me. Pushing me around like that."

Sam shrugged, which made Tripper even angrier. ". . . treating me like a baby. Taking over in the shoe store," she went on furiously. "Acting like such a big shot. *Talking about my feet behind my back!*"

It sounded so ridiculous, Tripper burst out laughing.

"Nice boots," Sam said. "Good fit, too."

"Sam," Tripper said. "I promise I'll get you back for this."

"Good," Sam said with a grin.

They passed the office of the *Tico Times.*

"I'd like to go in there," Sam said. "I'd like to see if I could talk to the reporter who did that article on parrot smuggling."

Sam went into the newspaper office and the rest of them waited outside.

"We must all be a little hungry," Alonso said. "I know *I* am hungry."

Alonso led Carlos and Tripper to a soda bar and everyone ordered a drink called *batidos.* It turned out to be a fruit milkshake. Tripper couldn't finish her papaya milkshake so Alonso offered to finish it for her.

"But you've already had three pineapple ones," Tripper couldn't help saying.

"Everyone say I have a very healthy appetite," Alonso said proudly. "I do a lot of workout. I keep my muscles strong."

To their surprise Alonso started doing push-ups on the sidewalk. He was still doing them when Sam joined Carlos and Tripper.

"Carlos," Sam said. "Where did Leroy say we were supposed to meet him?"

"At a cafe called Key Largo," Carlos said. "At five o'clock."

"Well, I did speak to the reporter. His name is Chris Wright, and he's very nice. He said that's where he usually goes after work. We might see him there. He's working on a big story. About an hour ago a cruising yacht ran aground near Puerto Quepos to the southwest of here. Then it exploded."

"Was anyone hurt?" Tripper asked.

"No," Sam said. "The crew had already abandoned the boat and disappeared. After the explosion they found that the boat had been carrying drugs, illegal arms. . . ." He paused and looked at Tripper. "There were also at least fifty dead parrots floating in the water."

"Sounds like the crew wanted to destroy the evidence," Tripper said.

Alonso finished his push-ups and jogged over to them.

"Now I show you some more sights," he said.

He took them wandering through the Central Market — a market full of fruit stalls, leather goods, and beautiful hand-made baskets. Then they stopped at a small stationery store.

"I want to get a postcard for Binker," Sam said.

Alonso tried to help him. "This one is very nice. It shows the mountains in central Costa Rica. You will be interested to know — "

"Binker doesn't like landscapes," Sam said and he picked a postcard with a picture of ripe coffee beans.

Alonso turned to Tripper. "This Binker," he whispered. "She is the girl friend?"

"No," Tripper said. "He is Sam's dog. Sam always misses Binker when he goes on location."

Alonso watched Sam fill out the address

on the postcard and write a message to Binker. He was very impressed. He turned to Tripper again.

"The dogs in Costa Rica — they do not read."

Tripper smiled. She didn't know what to make of Alonso. Sometimes he seemed so smart — so full of facts. Other times he seemed so gullible; he would believe anything.

"I'll mail it for you when we pass the post office," Alonso told Sam.

"Thanks." Sam handed the postcard to Alonso.

Key Largo was in an old colonial mansion set back from the street. It was surrounded by a garden.

As they turned onto the path that led to the entrance, Tripper said to Sam, "Did you notice how many people on the street smiled at us? It is a city full of smiles. I've never seen so many friendly people."

"Except for two," Sam muttered.

"Huh?" Tripper said.

"The two thugs who have been following us for the last hour don't look so friendly."

Key Largo

From their table by the window they could see the thugs standing outside on the sidewalk. Both men were wearing wrap-around sunglasses and Hawaiian shirts with palm trees on them.

"Maybe they're actors," Sam whispered to Tripper. "Maybe they're extras on the movie set."

Tripper agreed. The thugs seemed to fit right in. She felt as if she had stepped right into a scene from a spy movie. Key Largo had an air of mystery and foreign intrigue with its dark-paneled walls, dim light bulbs, and big fans turning slowly on the ceiling. There were posters from Humphrey Bogart movies on the wall.

"Very famous place," Alonso told them. "Many Americans come here."

Sam spotted Chris Wright coming in the

door. Chris Wright waved to Sam and came over to their table.

"I don't have much time," he said apologetically. "I've decided to go to Puerto Quepos and follow up this story on the cruising yacht MARAUDER."

"Do they know who owned the boat?" Sam asked.

"Well, there's some confusion about the registry," Chris told him. "Up until six months ago MARAUDER belonged to Barry Tours, but it was sold to a private individual."

Alonso sat up straight. "What happened?" he asked.

Chris told him what they knew so far.

"But I don't understand," Alonso said. He seemed to have lost some of his bounciness.

"Neither do I," Chris said cheerfully. "That's why I'm going down there."

After he had said good-bye, Sam poked Tripper. "They're still out there," he said.

Tripper looked out at the thugs.

"The one on the right looks sort of familiar," Tripper said. "That one — the one with the dark hair."

"Alonso," Sam said. "Have you ever seen either of those two men before?"

Alonso had been staring off into space. He glanced out the window. For a moment he looked startled. Then he shook his head. "Probably they are tourists," he said.

"Tourists?" Tripper and Sam looked at each other.

Alonso seemed anxious to change the subject. "You will be interested to know that everyone comes in here. San José — it is like a small town. Families come here. Government workers, businessmen, journalists. . . ."

"Smugglers?" Sam asked. Sam's ears were tuned in to a conversation at the next table. Two seedy-looking Americans had their heads together. They were speaking in an undertone. Tripper tried to listen, too, but their voices faded in and out. She could only get pieces of the conversation.

". . . I think we understand each other. . . ."

". . . want to play ball. . . ."

". . . if you get my meaning. . . ."

It certainly sounded as if they were doing some kind of illegal business.

"Oh yes," Alonso said. "Smugglers come in here. Undercover agents, too. You can't always tell the difference."

"I wish we didn't look so clean-cut and

wholesome," Tripper whispered to Sam.

Sam was listening to the conversation with a puzzled expression on his face.

"What are they talking about?" Tripper asked.

"Toasters," Sam said. "Food blenders."

Carlos leaned forward and said, "I've heard household appliances are hot items down here. They're very much in demand."

Tripper felt a little let down. Smuggling toasters didn't sound very thrilling. She looked up and saw the two thugs standing in the doorway. They were looking the place over. Then they chose a table by the wall near them and sat down without saying a word.

"They keep looking at you," Sam said to Alonso. "Are you sure you don't know them?"

Alonso said, "Maybe I play soccer with them one time. I do not know."

The waiter came over and they all ordered lemon drinks. While they waited for Leroy, Carlos began discussing how they would work together as a second unit film crew in the jungle.

"Tripper," Carlos said, "do you think you'll be able to follow focus for me while I'm shooting?"

"Of course," Tripper said. She noticed that the two thugs had ordered frothy pink drinks with strawberries and pineapple slices on top. Tripper thought it was a silly drink for thugs to order. She was disappointed in them.

Carlos went on. "But how do you feel about loading the magazines?" he asked Tripper.

"Fine," Tripper said. She'd seen Carlos loading the film holders millions of times. "You can go over it with me tonight."

Carlos turned to Sam. "Are you going to bring the shotgun?" Shotgun was another name for the long rifle mike.

One of the thugs suddenly choked on his frothy pink drink. It spilled on the table.

The place had suddenly become very quiet except for the hum of the big fans. Everyone seemed to be listening to their conversation.

"What's the matter?" Tripper whispered. "Did we say something wrong?"

Suddenly Carlos laughed. "Shotgun. Magazines. Everyone thinks we're talking about guns!"

The smugglers at the next table were staring at them. Tripper felt an apology was needed.

"We're just talking about making a documentary film," she said to the smugglers. "We didn't mean to scare you."

"Tripper!" Sam said, but it was too late. Tripper was now apologizing to the thugs.

" . . . and we're terribly sorry we made you spill your nice drink." Tripper stopped and stared at one of the thugs. "Hey, wait a minute. I know you!" she said. "You're Ted Barry's butler. What are you doing in Costa Rica? *And what have you done to your hair? You dyed it black.*"

Ted Barry's butler took off his dark glasses and glared at Tripper. Then he said something to Alonso in rapid Spanish.

Alonso looked very nervous. "I have to leave you now," he told Carlos, Tripper, and Sam. "Mr. Barry — he want to see me right now. Very important."

The three of them watched as Alonso was escorted a bit roughly out of Key Largo by the two men. "I pick you up tomorrow," Alonso called over his shoulder. "I pick you up and take you to the jungle. Do not worry."

But Alonso was worried — especially when he saw the big black limousine waiting for him around the corner. Ted Barry was sitting in the backseat. Alonso climbed in beside him and began to fidget.

"Well, it looks like we goofed, didn't we, Alonso?" Ted Barry was smiling, and Alonso was happy he was not angry about the MARAUDER. Besides, the verb "to goof" was not in Alonso's vocabulary yet. He settled back into the seat of the air-conditioned limousine.

"Alonso, Alonso, Alonso." Ted Barry was still smiling.

"I do not understand how it happened," Alonso told Mr. Barry. "My uncle in Quepos tell me this man is a very highly qualified sea captain. I do not understand why he run aground."

"Is that so?" Mr. Barry asked. "Oh, yes, there is one other thing. Didn't you tell me this sea captain was going to change the name of the boat and completely rebuild it?"

"Maybe he forget," Alonso said. He enjoyed riding in air-conditioned limousines and wondered where he was going.

"Maybe he forget," Ted Barry repeated, nodding his head. "In any case we lost a very expensive shipment — very expensive."

"Oh yes," Alonso said, "and the poor

little parrots we borrow from the reserve at Carrara will not be able to take part in your captive breeding program."

"So true," Mr. Barry said. "Now we don't want to mess up again, do we, Alonso?"

Alonso shook his head. He did not altogether understand the secret research project he was helping Mr. Barry with. All he understood was that they were borrowing birds from the jungles of Central and South America so that they could be bred. Then there would be plenty of parrots for little children to have as pets. One day those birds and many others would be returned to the jungles to repopulate the bird population . . . or something like that.

Alonso did understand, however, that the birds he borrowed last week from the rain forest at Carrara would never be returned.

"Now," Ted Barry said. "It might be a good idea for us to rethink this Corcovado plan."

Then Mr. Barry explained to Alonso that Alonso would not be going with the film crew to the jungle at Sirena, but to Puerto Jiménez on the east coast of the Osa Peninsula. Mr. Barry would take care of the arrangements in the jungle himself.

"However, in Puerto Jiménez you will make contact with a driver named Jorge who has been recommended to us. You will arrange the pickup of the shipment with him," Mr. Barry went on. "From what I understand a boat cannot land near the jungle station. The Pacific Ocean is too rough there."

"I do not go with the film crew to the jungle?" Alonso was very disappointed. "I just hire a driver?"

"I'm afraid so," Ted Barry said. "Except for one other little job."

"What's that?" Alonso asked.

"You will be doing a little baby-sitting," Ted Barry said with a smile.

Just then Alonso felt something crackling in the back pocket of his tennis shorts. He pulled out the postcard with the picture of the ripe coffee beans.

"Oh no!" Alonso said. "I forget to mail the postcard to Binker!"

"Who is Binkum?" Ted Barry asked.

When Alonso told Mr. Barry that Sam had a dog who could read, Mr. Barry was very interested. He said *he* would make sure Binker got the postcard, ". . . by special mail," he promised. "And now we go up to the house."

Alonso was pleased. He had been to Mr. Barry's house in the suburbs only once before. It was very large and well-guarded. There were beautiful birds in cages from all over the world, getting ready to take part in Mr. Barry's secret breeding program. There was even a Harpy eagle, one of the rarest birds in the world.

Alonso found himself wondering what time dinner was served in the Barry household. He certainly hoped he would arrive in time for a little bite to eat. . . .

Bad News

The Hotel Los Portales was to the north-west of San José in an ancient Indian village called Escazu. It was a beautiful hotel spread out like a ranch on the top of a mountain.

When the second unit got back from the shopping trip, Tripper went straight to her room, which turned out to be an enormous suite.

There was a large living room with a big fireplace and a patio full of flowers and trees. The bedroom also had a private patio that overlooked the mountains. Sam's room was right next door and she could hear him playing his record player.

She took a bath in a sunken marble bathtub and put on her long white terry-cloth robe. Then she put on her boots again.

She wanted to break them in by tomorrow morning.

There was a knock at the door. It was a young man who introduced himself as Luis. Luis was a gardener who worked at the hotel. He offered to build her a fire in the fireplace.

"It gets chilly when the sun goes down," he said with a big smile. His English was excellent.

"Thank you," Tripper said. "I'd love a fire."

When Luis finished building the fire, he said, "Would you like anything? A cup of cocoa perhaps?"

"Well. . . ." Tripper was very fussy about cocoa. She usually traveled with her own brand of extra dark cocoa that came from Holland. "Where is the cocoa from?" she asked Luis.

Luis smiled. "Cocoa beans grow in Costa Rica," he said. "Cocoa is one of our major products."

Tripper blushed. "A cup of cocoa would be very nice," she said.

The cocoa was excellent. Luis added some more wood to the fire. "I hear you are going to the Osa Peninsula," he said to Tripper.

Tripper nodded. She felt cozy and very sleepy.

"Very few Costa Ricans have been there," Luis said. He turned around and looked at Tripper. His eyes were sparkling. "I think it will be the adventure of your life. . . ."

Breakfast was served on the hotel terrace the next morning. From the terrace they could see the mountains and a volcano in the distance.

Roger Tripper joined the second unit for breakfast, but he kept his eye on the rest of the film crew as they set up to shoot the first day of the international wildlife convention.

Dr. Maria Vasquez stopped at their table to say hello. She was very nervous about the paper she was about to deliver. . . .

" . . . but at least I know," she said with her slow smile, "that as soon as it is over I will be flying out to Corcovado with my new friends."

Carlos, Tripper, and Sam ordered the breakfast *tipico*. The typical Costa Rican breakfast consisted of two fried eggs, rice and beans, fried bananas, yogurt, fresh fruit, and tortillas.

Just as the food arrived, Alonso arrived.

"We must all be very hungry," he said as he picked up a menu. "I know *I* am hungry."

Roger Tripper tried to hide his smile. "Won't you join us for breakfast, Alonso?" he asked.

To everyone's surprise Alonso had *two* typical breakfasts. But Tripper was so excited about the trip to the jungle, she couldn't eat anything.

"I understand you are familiar with the Osa Peninsula," Tripper's father said to Alonso.

"Oh yes," Alonso said, reaching for another tortilla. "I visit there many times. My uncle — he live there. Very nice man."

Just then Luis came over to the table.

"There is a telephone call from New York City," he said. He turned to Sam. "I believe it is from your mother."

Sam looked at his watch. "It's eight o'clock," he said. "That means it's nine o'clock in New York. I don't get it. Mom should be at work now."

Sam's mother was a librarian at the main branch of the New York Public Library. She had to be at work at eight-thirty.

"There's a phone at the desk here," Luis said.

Tripper followed Sam to the desk at the entrance to the terrace. Sam picked up the phone.

"Hi, Mom, is there anything wrong?" He listened a moment. Then he shouted, "What?"

"What happened?" Tripper was scared.

"Are you at the medical center now?" Sam asked. *"Mom, I can't hear you!"*

Sam suddenly hung up the phone. "She's calling back," he said. "We have to get a better connection."

"What's wrong?" Tripper looked at Sam's face and knew something terrible had happened.

"All I know," Sam said, "is that Binker was hit by a car this morning — a hit-and-run driver — in Riverside Park."

"Oh no!" Tripper noticed that Luis was standing by. He looked almost as if *he* was about to cry.

"It's his dog," Tripper explained. Luis nodded.

Sam just stared at the phone, waiting for it to ring.

Tripper said, "It doesn't make sense. There are no cars *in* Riverside Park."

"I know." Sam's green eyes flashed with anger. "Believe it or not, a car drove right up on the plaza by the Soldiers and Sailors Monument. It was almost as if they were aiming right for Binker!"

Tripper was afraid to ask if Binker was dead. He couldn't be, she told herself. She felt terrible about all the mean thoughts she had ever had about Binker.

Just then Ted Barry came striding across the terrace. He was wearing a one-piece plum-colored flightsuit.

The phone rang. Sam froze. Luis picked it up and said something in Spanish. He handed the phone to Sam.

"It's the international operator," he said. "Your call is ready. It sounds like a better connection."

Sam picked up the phone. "I'm here, Mom," he said. He listened.

Tripper was watching Sam's face so intently it took a few seconds for her to realize that Ted Barry was speaking to her.

"I heard the bad news," he said in a low, sympathetic voice. "It's a terrible thing, and I just want you to tell your friend that I would be more than happy to pay for an airplane ticket so that he can be with his pet in his hour of need."

"We don't know Binker's condition yet," Tripper said impatiently. She wondered how Ted Barry had heard the news so quickly.

Suddenly Sam shouted, "Really?" and let out a Texas war whoop. "He's all right!" he yelled at Tripper. "The vet just gave Mom the report. Binker's fine, believe it or not."

When he got off the phone, Luis shook his hand. Ted Barry suddenly lost interest in the whole incident and went over to talk to Tripper's father.

"The wheels completely missed him," Sam said. "He was just stunned for a while. Mom says he's completely recovered. She said Binker was just as alert as usual."

Tripper couldn't help wondering what *that* meant, but she felt so happy she wanted to hug Sam.

All at once the terrace was crowded with people. The convention was starting. Tripper saw Dr. Vasquez going into the conference room.

Roger Tripper came over. "I've got to go inside," he said, "but everything is all set. As soon as Dr. Vasquez delivers her paper,

Leroy is taking you to a small airfield near-by. Ted Barry has two planes waiting for you there, so there will be plenty of room for all the equipment."

He gave Tripper a big hug. "Have fun," he said, "and make sure Ted Barry doesn't sneak into any of the jungle shots."

"Right, Dad," Tripper said, and she hugged him back.

Tripper and Sam stood on the small airfield and watched the planes being loaded.

"Ted Barry sure has a lot of fancy luggage," Tripper whispered. "I'll bet he packed his hair blower, too."

The two planes were tiny four-seater Cessnas. Tripper was surprised to find that she, Sam, and Alonso were all going in one plane.

"But shouldn't I be going with Carlos?" she asked. "I think I have to help him with the aerial shots of the jungle."

Ted Barry smiled and said, "Safety first. These planes are so light, balance is essential. Your cameraman says he can handle it."

Tripper and Sam watched as the first plane carrying Ted Barry, Carlos, and Dr. Vasquez took off. Then they climbed into the second plane with Alonso. Alonso sat in the front with the pilot, and strapped himself into the seat.

The plane took off almost immediately.

Alonso was very excited. He had never ridden in such a tiny plane. He craned his neck around so that he would get a good view of the tallest mountain in Costa Rica when they flew over it.

Just then he caught a glimpse of Tripper and Sam's faces. They were staring at the pilot.

"Oh, do not worry," Alonso said. "Ralph is a highly qualified pilot. He flies very well."

The pilot was Ted Barry's butler.

The Back Way

"Maybe a taxi comes to take us into Puerto Jiménez," Alonso said, and he began practicing some karate exercises on the narrow landing strip in the middle of a grassy field.

"You know, Sam," Tripper said, "it's going to be a bit difficult to take a taxi from this airport."

Tripper was sitting on her knapsack in the hot sun. Sam was studying a map of the Osa Peninsula that he had spread out on the grass.

". . . and the reason it will be difficult to take a taxi from this airport," Tripper went on, "is that I don't see any airport."

"An airport is just a landing field," Sam muttered. "Technically you don't need buildings to call it an airport."

"That's good," Tripper said. "Because

there are no buildings, and I don't see a whole lot of taxi stands, either."

Ted Barry's butler had complained of engine problems and dropped them off near a place called Puerto Jiménez on the east coast of the Osa Peninsula. He said he had to go back to San José to have the engine checked out.

"The jungle station at Sirena is on the west coast of the Peninsula," Sam said. "On the Pacific side. We're on the Golfo Dulce."

They both looked over at Alonso, who was slicing the air with his hands and leaping about while he yelled something that sounded like "Aiiaiiiyoo."

"This is ridiculous," Sam said. "Alonso!" he called. But Alonso was deep in concentration.

Tripper and Sam were forced to wait until he finished his routine. He gave a few final grunts and jogged over to them.

"The taxi he is not here yet?" Alonso asked.

"We're going to have to walk," Sam said. "From the map it looks like it's only about a ten-minute walk to the center of Puerto Jiménez."

"I meet you downtown then," Alonso said, and he jogged off.

Tripper and Sam were sitting on the edge of a wooden porch. They were the center of attention in the small town. Some of the local people tried to help them, but Tripper and Sam couldn't understand them.

"I guess this must be downtown Puerto Jiménez," Sam said.

Puerto Jiménez was a hot, dusty town. It looked just like a town out of the Old West. Horses were tied to hitching posts along the row of wooden stores. There wasn't a vehicle of any kind in sight. Alonso was nowhere to be seen.

"Remind me to switch to Spanish next semester," Sam muttered, "when we get back to the States."

"*If* we get back," Tripper said.

A small boy came up to Tripper and handed her a box of wooden matches.

"*Graçias,*" Tripper said, and she smiled at him.

Other people did not look so friendly.

"Looks like there are some pretty rough characters around here," Sam said.

Many people were watching them with suspicion. Just then a blue pickup truck came rumbling into town. Everyone turned around to stare at it.

Alonso climbed down from the back. He waved to Tripper and Sam. "I be with you in just a moment," he called.

He went around the truck to talk to the driver. They seemed to be discussing money. Tripper kept hearing the word *la lapa* over and over.

When Alonso finally joined them, he seemed very cheerful. "That is Jorge," he said.

"What were you talking about?" Tripper asked. "What does *la lapa* mean?"

"Oh, I just ask him how is my uncle who lives on the Peninsula," Alonso said.

"But what does *la lapa* mean?" Tripper asked.

"It means 'uncle,' " Alonso said.

"I thought the Spanish word for 'uncle' was *tio*," Sam said.

"Oh it is," Alonso said, "but *la lapa* is — how do you call it — the Spanish word of endearment for 'uncle.' "

Jorge was still sitting in his truck staring at Tripper and Sam. He looked mean and sullen.

"Jorge tell me that maybe we get a plane to the jungle tomorrow," Alonso said.

"What?" Sam lost his temper. "Alonso, don't you understand? Tripper and I are part of a film crew. *We can't lose a day of shooting.*"

Alonso cleared his throat nervously. "You will be interested to know," he began, "that Puerto Jiménez is a very interesting town with a very interesting history. It has always been a famous gold prospecting town. You will be interested to know that the largest piece of gold ever found in the world was found on the Osa Peninsula — "

Sam interrupted. "Wait a minute. What about Jorge? He has a truck. Maybe he can drive us to the jungle station. Ask him, Alonso. Tell him we'll pay him."

"But. . . ." Alonso had orders from Ted Barry. He had been told to stay in Puerto Jiménez with the two North American kids and then return the next day to San José.

"Ask him," Sam said again.

Alonso thought about it. He had done what he was supposed to do. Jorge would pick up a shipment of parrots from the jungle the following week. Maybe he could go to the jungle after all. He could baby-sit for Tripper and Sam there. Ted Barry wouldn't mind as long as they stayed out of the way of his secret research project.

"I ask Jorge," Alonso said.

Alonso went over to talk to the driver. Jorge said he would drive them, but it would cost them a lot of money. The roads were bad; his truck would need many repairs after the journey.

But when Alonso heard the price Jorge was demanding, he shrugged and went back to tell Sam what Jorge had said.

"No good," Alonso said. "He want too many colons. More than one hundred dollars."

"That's fine," Sam said.

"But. . . ." Alonso couldn't believe it.

"Do you know how much it costs a film crew to lose an entire day of shooting?" Sam asked.

Alonso was pleased. "Then we go," he said. "But Jorge say we have to pay him the money first."

Sam paid the driver with the money Leroy had given him. Tripper and Sam climbed into the back of the blue pickup truck and Alonso sat in the cab with Jorge.

It was the roughest truck ride they had

ever been on. They had to hold on tight to the wooden slats as the truck plunged through rivers and climbed steep hills of rocks and dirt as they went south and then west along the coast of the Osa Peninsula.

But the scenery was wild and beautiful. As they were passing a lagoon, Sam said to Tripper, "Isn't it great that we *had* to come the back way? Otherwise we'd never get a chance to see anything like this in our life!"

Tripper agreed. "It's the most exciting ride I've ever been on."

They had been riding for three hours when the truck came to a sudden stop.

Alonso jumped out of the cab. Ahead of them was a small store with a sign that said CARATE.

"Well, here we are," Alonso said. "No more roads."

Sam was staring at his map. "But we're only at Carate!"

"Last stop," Alonso said. "Now we go for a little walk along the beach. No problem."

Tripper put on her knapsack and climbed off the truck. She stopped dead in her tracks and stared at the beach.

It was the wildest beach Tripper had

ever seen. There were sharp volcanic rocks, tangled fallen trees and branches. Deep pools of sea water were everywhere.

"Maybe the beach gets better up ahead," Alonso said a little nervously.

"Maybe it gets worse," Sam said. "Look, if we're only at Carate, we don't have a chance of making it to the jungle station before dark. It's almost five o'clock. The sun sets at six."

They heard the sound of a motor. The blue pickup truck had turned around and was heading back.

"Wait!" Sam yelled, but Jorge didn't stop. In no time at all the truck was out of sight.

The town of Carate was made up of the one little store and a few cabins behind it, which were used as a camp for gold prospectors.

Luckily, the owner of the camp turned out to be a Canadian who spoke English. His name was Bill, and he took Sam up to his cabin to show him some more maps.

Alonso and Tripper waited on the porch of the small store. Tripper felt quite weak. She wished she had eaten her breakfast. She felt worse when she realized that

Alonso hadn't mentioned food all day. Something must be worrying him.

Sam was gone for quite a while. When he returned, he looked grim. He spread a map out on the porch.

"Alonso," he said softly. "Come here. I want you to tell me what the name of this point means in English."

Alonso studied the map. "Ah," he said. "That is very interesting. Now, Salsipuedes is actually a combination of three Spanish words put together." Alonso had perked up. He loved explaining things to others.

"And what do those words mean?" Sam asked. Tripper was sure Sam already knew the answer. He was acting like a schoolteacher and it scared her.

Alonso cleared his throat. "Ahem," he began. "*Sal*— that means 'get out.' Now sometimes the word *sal* means 'salt,' but in this case. . . ."

"Go on," Sam said encouragingly.

". . . well, in this case, *sal* means 'get out'; *si* means 'if' and *puedes* means 'you can.'"

Alonso seemed quite pleased with himself.

"Now let's put it all together," Sam said

in his patient schoolteacher voice.

"It's called 'Point-Get-Out-*if*-You-Can.'"
Alonso waited for Sam to say something
like, "Very good, Alonso," but Sam seemed
to have lost interest in his star pupil.

Sam turned to Tripper. "Bill says there
is no passing that point at high tide.
There are huge boulders and rocks. The
sea comes right up to the jungle. There are
powerful currents. We would be dashed up
against the rocks."

Tripper looked at the map. "Couldn't we
just cut through the jungle?"

"There's no getting through the jungle
there," Sam told her.

" . . . and that is why they call the tropical rain forest on the Osa Peninsula a
living wall," Alonso explained. "There are
a great variety of plants and animal
species — "

Tripper interrupted. "What time is high
tide?" she asked Sam.

"Well, we have to wait until morning.
High tide is at eleven thirty-five. Bill says
we have to be past that point at least an
hour before high tide. Even if we leave at
daybreak we'll have trouble making it.
The sand gets very soft up ahead. . . ."

Sam stopped and looked at Tripper. "Bill

is very nice," he said. "He will find us beds for tonight, but only for tonight. There are gold miners coming in tomorrow. . . ."

"Did you tell him we would be happy to pay him?" Tripper asked.

"Money has nothing to do with it," Sam said sharply. "Food is scarce around here. For tonight we will be guests of the mining camp. If we stay any longer, we will be taking food from other people."

"Maybe we should go back," Tripper said.

"There is no way to get back," Sam told her. "Trucks hardly ever come here."

"Well, then. . . ." Tripper felt a little panicky. "We'd better call Leroy in San José and—"

"Tripper!" Sam said. "There are no telephones in this part of the Peninsula. What's more there is no radio communication at Carate. We can't even get a message to the station at Sirena to let them know where we are."

Sam studied Alonso for a few seconds. "Alonso," he said. "Why didn't you warn us about this before?"

Alonso began fidgeting with the buckle on his knapsack.

"Alonso," Sam went on. "Do you have

something you would like to tell us?"

Alonso mumbled something.

"I thought so," Sam said.

"Alonso has never been here before," Sam said.

"You've never been to the Osa Peninsula?" Tripper asked.

Alonso shook his head.

"Why did you tell us you had?" Tripper asked. "Why did you lie?"

"I do not lie," Alonso said indignantly. "I only try to help you."

Bones on the Beach

The cook of the mining camp served them dinner in a small room with windows overlooking the wild beach and the Pacific Ocean.

Sam ate quietly. Alonso had already finished. He was looking hungrily at Tripper's plate. She hadn't even touched her dinner. Every once in a while Wilhelmina, the cook, looked over at Tripper from behind the counter of the small kitchen.

Suddenly Sam looked up. "Tripper," he said, "I don't think you're going to make it."

"Of course we're going to make it," Tripper said.

"I didn't say we; I said you," Sam said desperately. "You won't be able to keep up. Do you know what the sun is going to be like on that beach? We're not prepared for anything. No food; no medical equipment; no camping gear. Not even a decent canteen."

"What makes you think that I'm the one who won't be able to keep up?" Tripper was furious. At the same time she felt so weak, she was afraid she wouldn't even be able to pick up her fork. If only she had eaten breakfast in San José.

Sam went on. "No one can rescue anyone else on that beach," he said. "No one should try it. If any one of us tries, two people will die instead of one."

"Now, just a minute," Tripper said. "Let's say I'm lying on the beach exhausted. Are you telling me that you would just walk away and leave me there?"

Sam didn't answer. He wouldn't look at Tripper.

All at once Tripper knew the answer. She knew Sam too well. A horrible picture came to her mind: the rugged beach, her bones and Sam's bones lying there, bleaching in the sun — and in the distance she could see Alonso jogging off into the west.

Alonso said casually to Tripper, "If you don't want your dinner. . . ."

"Don't touch her food!" Sam said.

"Tripper, eat your dinner. You need the strength."

"I'll eat if you leave me alone," Tripper whispered.

But even after Alonso and Sam had left the dining room, Tripper couldn't eat. She was having trouble swallowing.

Wilhelmina came from behind the counter and sat down across from Tripper. She pointed to the sun that was rapidly setting over the Pacific Ocean and said something to Tripper in Spanish.

Tripper looked at Wilhelmina and thought she had one of the most beautiful faces she had ever seen. Good company for my last night on earth, she found herself thinking. She looked out at the sun setting over the wild Pacific beach.

Wilhelmina pointed to the sun again. Then she said very slowly, "The ... sun ... is ... a ... girl ... lion."

Tripper smiled at Wilhelmina. She wondered if that was a legend around here. But it didn't matter. Suddenly she felt tears rolling down her cheeks, dripping into her rice and beans. Wilhelmina just sat there quietly while Tripper cried. She seemed to understand everything.

After a while, Tripper took a deep breath and began eating her rice and beans.

Sam was sitting on a bench outside the small dining room talking to Bill.

"Guess what," he said to Tripper. "We're in luck. Bill found us some horses for tomorrow morning. The owner of the horses is going with us. We leave at daybreak."

Tripper was first on the beach the next morning. The horse guide followed, leading a pack horse. Then came Sam, and then Alonso.

Tripper had never ridden a horse like Bayito before. Bayito was a small yellow-brown horse who didn't seem used to having a rider. She stumbled a lot and often went so close to the rocks, Tripper had to swing her leg around.

"Don't let her get away with that," Sam called. "She's doing it on purpose."

"Well, I don't think she's doing it to be *mean*." Tripper felt she had to defend Bayito.

During the first part of the trip, they saw many people on the rocks panning for gold. The jungle got thicker and the sand along the beach got softer. Bayito did not like soft sand. She stopped again and again.

Tripper saw Sam look up at the sun. He seemed worried. The horse guide seemed worried, too. He got off his horse and went to speak to Alonso.

"He says there is a path here that goes through the jungle," Alonso translated. "We should take it. If we go along the beach, we will not make Point Salsipuedes before the high tide. The sand is too soft."

Bayito did better in the jungle, but Tripper had to duck the low branches. When they got back to the beach, the sun seemed very hot after the coolness of the jungle.

By now Tripper had lost all sense of time. They came to a difficult stretch of rocks and boulders. Bayito slipped a number of times. Up ahead she saw Sam get off his horse. Everyone was taking a rest. Tripper caught up and climbed off Bayito.

"What's going on?" She looked at their faces. "You mean we made it?" she asked. "We passed Point Get-Out-*if*-We-Can?"

Sam nodded. "It should be only two more hours to the jungle station at Sirena."

* * *

Another hour went by and the beach had improved. All at once Tripper saw the horse guide stop. Right ahead of them was a rushing river.

"It's got to be the Rio Claro," Sam said. "We're very near the camp."

The guide seemed puzzled. There seemed to be no way to cross the river. He called to Alonso, who got off his horse.

"He is surprised," Alonso said. "He hasn't been up this way for a long time." Alonso went over to the pack horse and repacked the knapsacks. Tripper suddenly realized he was doing that so that his knapsack would be on top — so it wouldn't get wet. "Hey!" she said, but just at that moment, Tripper saw the guide lead his horse into the river, followed by the pack horse and Alonso on horseback. . . .

Bayito started to follow.

"No!" Sam called. "Follow me."

Tripper looked up. Sam had chosen a way across a narrow rocky ledge. It looked too difficult for Bayito.

"It's okay," Tripper called. "I don't mind getting a little wet."

But the rushing water of the river was

already up to Bayito's belly and Tripper's jeans were soaking wet.

Bayito stopped. She wouldn't move. Sam was standing on the steep bank on the other side. He had gotten off his horse.

"Tripper!" he yelled. "Get your horse out of there right now! Right this minute!"

"Look Sam," Tripper said. "Bayito probably has some very good reason for stopping. I'm sure she will go when she is ready."

The guide was now pulling the pack horse up the bank on the other side. Tripper saw Sam's boots fall into the water. Alonso had done a poor job of retying them onto the saddle.

"I'll get them!" Tripper called.

"No!" Sam said. "Stay on your horse and do what I say. Kick her. Kick her hard!"

At this point Tripper knew she had to choose between horse sense and human sense. She looked at Sam's face. He seemed to know something she didn't know. She kicked Bayito very hard. Bayito went a few steps and stopped at the steep bank.

Sam slid a few feet down the bank and grabbed Bayito's reins.

"Hold on tight, Tripper," he said. "Don't fall off."

Tripper grabbed Bayito around the neck and Sam pulled. Bayito stumbled up the bank.

Sam looked relieved. He got back on his horse. "Let's go," he said.

"But what about your boots?" she asked.

"Too late," Sam said. "Forget them."

Tripper looked back at the rushing water of the Rio Claro.

"Sam," she said quietly. "What are those white things flipping around in the water?"

But Sam was out of earshot.

What is white and flips around in the water? Tripper was still working on her little riddle when she saw a sign almost hidden by the creeping vines of the jungle.

The sign said ESTAÇION SIRENA.

Tripper felt a thrill go through her body. She forgot everything except the fact that they had arrived. They had made it!

An hour later Tripper and Sam were sitting on the porch of the jungle station. Their clothes were drying in the sun.

Everyone had been surprised to see them. Ted Barry had been especially surprised, but he smiled a big smile and said, "Alonso, may I have a word with you?"

Tripper looked up and saw a scarlet macaw in a high tree. There was another tree full of spider monkeys. The sun felt warm. She closed her eyes and listened to the loud buzzing of the cicadas.

Sam was deep in conversation with Manuel, a forest ranger who was in charge of the station.

"Well, I got suspicious," she heard Sam say, "when I saw all those dead sardines that had been chased up along the beaches."

"You were very lucky," Manuel said. "The Rio Claro is full of them at high tide. Needless to say, there is no swimming around here."

Suddenly Tripper opened her eyes wide and said, "Sharks!"

Jungle Sounds

The sleeping quarters at Station Sirena were above the porch of the main building. Cots were lined up on a long wooden platform with supporting beams and a roof, but no walls.

"I hope we don't do any sleepwalking," Tripper said as she and Sam hung the mosquito netting over their cots.

Just then they heard a series of very odd sounds. Tripper peeked over the edge of the platform. She sighed. "Alonso is showing off his bird calls. How ridiculous!"

"I don't think he's fooling the jungle," Sam said.

Manuel showed them around the jungle station and introduced them to some of the scientists who were working on the reserve.

Scientists came to the Corcovado Reserve

from all over the world to study tropical plants and animals. There were even laboratories on the ground floor of the main building where they could examine the specimens they collected.

"We have an electric generator," Manuel told them, "but it is only turned on for a few hours at night — just for the electric light bulbs. I had to tell Mr. Barry he was not allowed to use his electric hair dryer."

"I'll bet he was upset," Tripper said.

Manuel took them to the dining room, which was in a small wooden cabin about fifty yards away from the main building. Carlos and Dr. Vasquez sat with them while they ate lunch. But Tripper and Sam didn't talk much about the trip. They were too hungry and very happy just to be there.

Alonso ate quickly and stood up. He stretched his arms and patted his stomach. "Well," he announced, "now that I get you to the jungle safe and sound. . . ."

Tripper and Sam tried not to laugh.

". . . I take a few days off," Alonso went on. "I look around the jungle. Do some exercise. Make my muscles strong. Will you be able to get along without me to help you?"

"Sure," Sam said a little too quickly.

"Then I go now and change into my jogging suit," Alonso said.

Tripper and Sam were delighted. From then on they only saw Alonso at mealtime. And, over the next couple of days, they saw very little of Ted Barry. He had told everyone that he wanted to use his time at Corcovado to "touch base with Nature."

Tripper did get a glimpse of him one afternoon.

The second unit had gone out to film the flight of the scarlet macaw. Scarlet macaws seemed to be the royalty of the jungle. Their voices had a great range of expression. Their angry shrieks were enough to keep predators away from their young.

Carlos, Sam, and Tripper were setting up across a clearing from a dead nesting tree. Carlos had put the movie camera on a tripod. Sam had his headphones on and Tripper could tell by the faraway look in his eyes that he was concentrating hard on the sounds around them.

Tripper was checking the focus on the telephoto lens. Through the long lens she saw Ted Barry a long way off, talking to a man with a red beard. She figured the man was one of the forest rangers. He was carrying a rifle. Only the rangers were allowed to carry rifles on the reserve.

"Are you ready?" Carlos asked.

"I'd like to try following focus," Tripper said, and she put the whole incident out of her mind.

Carlos nodded to Sam, and Sam signaled that the tape recorder was rolling by circling his finger in the air. Just then, high up in the trees, a scarlet macaw gave a great leap that was part of its take-off and spread its magnificent wings. Carlos tilted the camera up and filmed the scarlet macaw as it soared into flight.

"Imagine wanting to teach a scarlet macaw to talk," Tripper said that night at dinner. She was sitting with Manuel and some of the other scientists. "They already seem to have quite a lot to say."

"We are lucky here," Manuel told her. "We have a population of about two hundred pairs of scarlet macaws, but not long ago there were thousands of them. I'm afraid the scarlet macaw is becoming extinct. This is the last retreat of *la lapa*."

"*La lapa?*" Tripper asked. Where had she heard that word before?

"*La lapa* is our word for scarlet macaw," Manuel explained.

"I see." Tripper thought for a moment. Then she said brightly, "And I understand it is also the Spanish word of endearment for 'uncle.'"

Manuel seemed a little puzzled. Just then he was called to the radio. Roger Tripper was calling from the Park Service in San José. Tripper went into Manuel's office.

"Everything's fine!" she told her father. "You ought to see the footage we're getting!" She didn't want to talk too long; it was a government radio. "No, Dad," she said. "We haven't seen a jaguar yet."

The next morning while it was still dark, Carlos, Tripper, and Sam went with Dr. Vasquez to wait on a hill overlooking a stream. It was here that Dr. Vasquez had observed jaguars on earlier trips.

"I can't promise you anything," Dr. Vasquez said again and again. "Jaguars are lone animals who hunt at night. I have come across them at twilight and very early in the morning, but we will be lucky if we see one."

"Will a jaguar attack a human being?" Sam asked.

"All large cats are dangerous," Dr. Vasquez said, "but remember, we are not

104

their usual prey. However, we should never get too close. If a jaguar finds you too close, he is certain to attack. Some people call this 'the radius of danger.' "

"How large is this 'radius of danger'?" Sam asked. "How many feet?"

Dr. Vasquez laughed. "I'm afraid it's up to the jaguar."

They waited for a long time. The jaguar didn't show up.

That afternoon after lunch, Tripper sat on the porch of the jungle station and watched Sam play frisbee with Manuel on the field in front of the main building. She knew Sam wasn't playing frisbee just for fun. He wanted to keep his mind off the chigger bites that covered his ankles and legs. He had been suffering without his boots. Tripper felt guilty that she had a very nice pair of boots — thanks to Sam — and he had none.

Sam had tried using heavy silver tape, which filmmakers call gaffer tape, to tape his pants to his running shoes, but it didn't do much good. He tried very hard not to scratch the bites.

Sam and Tripper went out that evening to record jungle sounds at dusk. They sat on a piece of driftwood at the edge of the jungle on the deserted beach that stretched along the Pacific Ocean.

Sam used two microphones to record. He held a microphone to each ear. "It's called bifonic recording," he said. "I'm trying to match the space between the ears. Sound always hits one ear a fraction of a second before it hits the other. This kind of recording is supposed to give the most natural sound."

Right at dusk it seemed as if someone had turned a switch. The jungle suddenly came alive with sounds.

Tripper sat quietly and watched the hermit crabs on the beach. Some were growing out of their old shells and were searching around for bigger shells to make into new homes. She felt very peaceful and content.

When Sam finished recording, she said, "We belong here, too — don't we? People belong in the jungle, too."

Sam nodded.

As soon as they got back to the sleeping platform, Sam noticed his roll of gaffer tape was missing.

"That's strange," Sam said. "It was right on my bed."

When Tripper went to get her pair of socks on the clothesline, they were missing, too.

They reported the missing gaffer tape to Manuel, but it was hard to believe that anyone would steal a pair of Tripper's socks.

That night they sat with Dr. Vasquez by the stream. They had been waiting for twenty minutes when they heard a low roar. They heard a slight movement in the bushes, but it was too dark to see anything. Afterward, they were very excited. They had been in the presence of a jaguar, and Sam had recorded it.

After dinner they played the tapes with the dusk recordings and the jaguar sounds. The scientists were very impressed with the bifonic recording and took turns listening with the headphones.

"I really just did that for fun," Sam said. "There is too much information here to work well in a film. On the screen the eye is already being directed by the camera. We expect to hear what the camera is seeing."

Then he played the recording of the jaguar. When Tripper heard the low roar again, the hairs on her neck stood on end.

Suddenly Manuel said, "Stop. Play that part again. Something's wrong."

"I know," Sam said. "I heard it, too."

Sam played the tape again. There was the sound of a chain saw in the distance.

"I don't understand," Dr. Vasquez said. "Why didn't we hear it at the time?"

"Because we were all listening for a particular sound," Sam said. "And when you are listening for a particular sound, you tend to block out all other sounds. We were all listening for the sound of the jaguar."

"Well, I certainly was," Dr. Vasquez said. She turned to Manuel. "But who would be using a chain saw?" she asked.

"A gold prospector," Manuel said. He seemed very angry. "They cut down trees to dam up rivers to pan for gold. They're not allowed on the reserve. Do you know what it means to cut down a single tree?"

Tripper and Sam shook their heads.

"A mating pair of scarlet macaws, for instance, might spend years searching for another nesting tree," Manuel explained. "And right now the gold prospectors are the biggest danger. I caught a man two weeks ago — a North American — and kicked him off the reserve. He was carrying a rifle, and I think he was shooting at parrots."

"Why would anyone do that?" Tripper asked.

Manuel's voice trembled with rage. "For target practice," he said.

"Well, well, well. We seem to be having a cozy little get-together." Ted Barry was standing in the doorway.

Suddenly Tripper remembered something. "I saw you talking to a man with a rifle yesterday," she said to Ted Barry. "That man with the red beard. I thought he was one of the rangers."

"He's no ranger," Manuel said sharply. "That's the man I'm talking about." He turned to Ted Barry. "What did he say to you?"

Ted Barry looked shocked. "I haven't the faintest idea what she's talking about."

"But I saw you," Tripper said, "through the telephoto lens."

Ted Barry laughed. "My dear girl," he said, "I think the jungle is getting to you."

Manuel stood up. "Look," he said, "it's too dark to go out looking now, but if anyone sees that man, let me know at once, and stay away from him. He's dangerous."

Ted Barry leaned over and murmured in Tripper's ear, "Seriously — some of the people here have been getting a little worried about you. A little less sun, perhaps. . . ."

Tracking

At three-thirty the next morning the second unit joined Dr. Vasquez in front of the sleeping quarters.

Dr. Vasquez whispered, "If we are going to see the jaguar at all, I have a feeling it will be this morning. Just my instinct."

"I'd like to try using a radio mike today," Sam said. "I want to place it near the spot where we heard the jaguar last night. Then we'll know at once when he's in the area and we'll be ready."

Dr. Vasquez liked that idea very much.

They waited while Sam tested both of his wireless mikes to make sure they were working. Tripper held her flashlight so he could see.

They were surrounded by darkness. The scientists were still asleep on the platform above. Even the howling monkeys hadn't woken up yet. The loudest sounds were the cicadas and Sam's voice quietly testing, "Wun . . . wun . . . wun. . . ."

Sam chose the mike that transmitted over Channel A on his receiver and put it into a small bag with a drawstring. He put the Channel B microphone in his pocket.

When they got to the stream, Sam tied the bag with the radio mike in it onto the branch of a fallen log. Then he climbed the hill to join the others and wait.

The jaguar was very considerate that morning.

As soon as it got light, the radio mike picked up a rustling in the bushes by the bank of the stream. Sam gave Carlos a signal and Carlos turned on the camera. The camera hardly made any noise.

A few seconds later a jaguar came down to the stream to fish. He slapped fish out of the water with his powerful paw. When he was done with his meal, he looked up at the spot where the film crew was sitting, as if to ask, "Well, how was that?" Then he strode off into the rain forest.

Carlos kept the camera rolling for a little while longer. Then he turned it off and took a deep breath.

Everyone just sat there in silence looking at one another. No one seemed to know what to say. Finally Dr. Vasquez said in a choked-up voice, "Do you think I might be able to get a print of that? I'd be happy to pay for it."

"Of course you can have a print," Carlos said.

"He looked at us!" Tripper felt like a stage-struck kid who had just seen a famous star come out of the dressing room. "He looked right at us!"

It was now six forty-five. Breakfast was served at seven.

"I'll go down and get the radio mike," Sam said. "I'll change the battery and meet you back in the dining room."

Sam was only halfway down the hill when he heard a loud purring over his headphones. Then he heard a series of crashes. Even the slightest touch on a microphone makes a loud noise, and he crouched down and peeked through the bushes to see what was going on.

Across the stream a young jaguar was playing with the bag on the string — the bag with the radio mike in it. He was play-

ing just the way a kitten would play —
batting it with his paw, watching it swing
and then batting it again.

Sam turned and looked up the hill, but
the rest of the film crew was gone. He
wanted to keep recording, but he had to
change tapes.

All at once he thought of Dr. Vasquez's
words, "radius of danger." He stopped
what he was doing and looked at the jaguar.

He wasn't a baby; he was what Dr.
Vasquez would call a juvenile. Right now
he looked cute and playful, but he was big
enough to be dangerous. And what about
his mother? Where was she?

Sam took off his headphones and listened.
For, despite all of Sam's interest in recording good sound, he knew that his own ears
were the most sensitive instruments he had
—better than any microphone that had
ever been invented.

He heard a faint click. Slowly he scanned
the bushes at the edge of the stream.

Suddenly he saw a glint of metal. A rifle
barrel was trained on the young jaguar.
Someone was lying in the bushes just
across the stream, about to shoot the
jaguar.

Sam took the empty reel off his tape recorder. He got to his feet and aimed for the spot behind the rifle — the spot where the person holding the rifle would be. Then, using his best frisbee form, he tossed the reel across the stream.

There was a yelp from the bushes and a man with a red beard scrambled up. The jaguar had disappeared.

The man was clutching the empty reel and staring at it. Then he looked across the stream. His eyes met Sam's. He reached for his rifle.

Sam threw himself down on the ground and lay flat. His heart was pounding.

Then he heard the prospector crashing away into the bushes, cursing wildly.

Sam knew he had to tell Manuel right away. He went down to the stream, grabbed the bag with his radio mike in it, and took off in the direction of the station.

But he was having trouble running. He looked down and saw he had a deep cut on his ankle. He had no idea how he had gotten it.

He stopped. Someone was coming along the path. There was no time to hide. A minute later Alonso appeared around the bend. He was wearing his knapsack. He stopped short when he saw Sam. He seemed confused. He looked as if he had been expecting to meet someone else.

Sam warned Alonso about the prospector.

"Oh, I am not afraid," Alonso said.

"But he's got a gun," Sam said.

"If I meet him, I just do my karate chop." Alonso demonstrated.

Sam studied Alonso for a few seconds. "Alonso," he said slowly, "why are you wearing your knapsack? Are you leaving?"

"Oh no," Alonso said quickly. "I just go for a jog. I carry my knapsack for weight."

"Wait a minute!" Sam was now very suspicious. "What about breakfast? You're missing breakfast."

"Oh, I do not feel like eating breakfast today," Alonso said. "I must hurry now."

Alonso missing breakfast? That was too much. Sam was sure Alonso was up to something. He blocked Alonso's way. "Wait, Alonso," Sam said. "Um . . . that knapsack doesn't look heavy enough. Let me see." Sam felt the knapsack. "No, you need more weight."

"I do?" Alonso asked.

"Yes," Sam said. "You ought to see the weights the joggers carry around in Central Park."

Sam found a rock and slipped it into the

bag with the radio mike. He tucked the bag into the back of Alonso's knapsack and kept talking.

". . . and in Riverside Park the joggers. . . ." Sam suddenly thought of Binker. *Binker had been hit by a car in Riverside Park.*

"Alonso," he said casually, "did you ever mail that postcard to Binker?"

"Oh, Ted Barry, he mailed it for me. He sent it by special mail. Didn't Binker get it?"

"Oh yes," Sam said. "He got it all right."

It seemed impossible that anyone would send a hit man after a dog, but Sam had a feeling that very shortly things would start to make sense. He stuck another rock in Alonso's knapsack.

"Oh, that is not heavy," Alonso said. "Not for me!"

Sam waited for Alonso to get out of sight. Now he could track Alonso without being seen. He would simply listen over his headphones and follow the signal being broadcast from the radio mike in Alonso's knapsack.

Sam put a new tape into his tape recorder and set off after Alonso.

The signal led him down a path that led

to the River Sirena. Then, over the head-phones, he heard Alonso say, "Well, I am here, but I do not understand why you tell me to bring socks and this tape."

"Maybe the nice man will show you." It was Ted Barry's voice. "Just give him the socks and the tape."

"It's very simple," a gruff voice said. Sam knew at once it was the voice of the gold prospector. "Just let me dig into my sack here."

Suddenly there was violent squawking. Sam heard Alonso gasp. "What are you doing?" Alonso asked. "You can't stuff little macaws into socks!"

"Sure I can," the prospector said. "I'm doing it, aren't I? They make cute little strait jackets."

Sam had the sickening picture in his head of baby macaws being stuffed into Tripper's socks.

"And now a little tape to tape up the cute little beaks."

The squawking stopped.

Sam heard Alonso ask, "Are you sure they are comfortable like that?"

"Of course," the prospector said. "It makes them feel real secure."

Sam moved closer. Through the forest he could see the dead nesting tree lying across the clearing. He could see empty nests and dead birds scattered on the ground. These were the birds who made their homes in the same tree as the scarlet macaws. But Sam knew that these birds would not bring in as much money at the pet stores.

He did not dare go any closer. Just then he heard Ted Barry say, "Where is the rest of the shipment? Where are you keeping the rest of the birds?"

There was no answer.

"Did you hear what I said?" Ted Barry asked.

"I hear these macaws bring in a lot of money." The gold prospector was talking again. "What do you think you'll get for these?"

"Oh, Mr. Barry he is not interested in the money," Sam heard Alonso say. "He breeds them in his house so children will be able to have pets and no one will have to steal them from the jungle."

"We wouldn't want anyone to steal little parrots from the jungle," the prospector said.

"Mr. Barry does not steal these macaws," Alonso said indignantly. "He just borrows them."

"That's enough!" Ted Barry said. Then he went on in an icy voice. "I asked you a question. Where are the rest of the birds you collected?"

Suddenly the prospector's voice became a whine. "Look, mister, something came up. I couldn't work as fast as usual. In a few days, maybe. . . ."

"In a few days . . ." Ted Barry repeated. Then Sam heard him shout, "You idiot!"

"Well, I guess I run along now," Alonso began nervously. "I'll just take the little parrots in my knapsack to Jorge. . . ."

"Two parrots?" Ted Barry asked. "What good are two parrots to me?"

"Yes, yes," Alonso went on. "I just tuck them in, but first I just take these weights out. Then I will run faster."

Sam froze. He heard the sound of a zipper over the headphones. Then he heard Alonso say, "Ha. Ha. Look what that boy put in my knapsack by mistake."

"Give that to me," Ted Barry snapped.

Sam knew he had to move fast. He had to get away. But his tape recorder would slow him down. He took the tape recorder off his shoulder and looked around for a place to hide it.

Sam heard Ted Barry's voice over his headphones again, but now it was smooth — confident — just like his tv commercials. "This is Ted Barry speaking. Don't worry, my dear boy, you won't get away from me. There is no place to hide. I repeat. . . . There is no place to hide. . . ."

Sam ripped the headphones off and quickly took the tape off the tape recorder and put it into his shoulder bag.

Nothing could happen to that tape. He had his evidence against Ted Barry. Now he knew Ted Barry wasn't dedicated to the preservation of wildlife; he was only after a profit.

Sam slipped the tape recorder under a bush and got down on his stomach. He began creeping through the underbrush. The cut on his ankle was quite painful now. If only he could reach that clearing. . . .

Slowly, inch by inch, he pulled himself along. It seemed to take forever.

There was a racket of macaws overhead. Sam decided to use that noise as a cover to make a break for the clearing. He stood up.

But he couldn't move. His shoulder bag

was caught on something. He pulled, but he couldn't seem to release it. When he turned around to untangle it, he saw the strap wasn't caught on a branch.

The gold prospector was holding it.

He pulled Sam close and whispered in his ear, "Well, if it isn't my favorite frisbee player."

Sam:
Endangered Species

Tripper could not understand why Sam did not show up for breakfast. Ted Barry did show up. He announced he was leaving for San José within the hour. A plane had been sent for. "Important business," he explained.

By eight o'clock Tripper was very worried about Sam. She checked all the buildings at the jungle station. She could hear the motor of a Cessna as it landed to pick up Ted Barry.

At nine o'clock Manuel said he would go with her to look for Sam.

There was no sign of Sam by the stream. They called his name again and again, but there was no answer. They searched in the direction of the River Sirena. Just before they reached the mouth of the river, they saw the nesting tree that had been cut down.

"We're going back to the station," Manuel said. "We will organize search teams."

The rangers did not have walkie-talkies to communicate between the search parties, so it was agreed that whoever found Sam first would fire a shot into the air with his rifle.

At ten A.M. they found Sam's tape recorder hidden under the leaves.

"Sam would never leave his tape recorder," Tripper said. "And he left the battery switch on! Sam wouldn't do that. Something's happened to him!"

"We'll find him," Manuel said gently. "He's probably all right. He hasn't been missing that long."

"You don't understand." Tripper felt tears burning in her eyes. "Sam has these habits, you see...."

Carlos put on the headphones and turned the knob of the tape recorder. "I hear a signal," he said. "The radio mike is somewhere around here."

The three of them followed the signal down the path to the mouth of the River

Sirena. They turned south on the beach. The signal got stronger.

When Tripper saw the cloth bag with the radio mike in it lying on the deserted beach, her heart sank. There were faint footprints in the sand, but the waves had washed over them. The tide was coming in. Tripper tried not to look into the sea. She didn't want to see those white shapes flipping around in the water.

It was now ten-fifteen. Manuel asked Tripper and Carlos to wait for him while he ran up to the main building. "I'm calling the Park Service in San José on the radio," he said. "I am going to request that they send search planes."

He looked at Tripper. "Please do not give up hope," Manual said. "We've found people many times before. It's very easy to get lost around here. I'm sure Sam knows to stay in one place and wait to be found. I'm sure he knows that he should just make himself comfortable and not move around. . . ."

Sam could not move. He was tied up like a mummy, with magnetic recording tape wrapped around him from his neck to his ankles. He was tied up with the tape containing the evidence against Ted Barry.

He could not see; he could not hear; and he could not talk. The prospector had found a good use for the silver gaffer tape. He had wrapped it around Sam's eyes, ears, and mouth. The hardest part for Sam was not being able to hear.

He had no idea where he was. He could feel damp sand under him and the vibrations of the tide, but that was all he knew.

Sam remembered a movie he had seen about hermit crabs — hermit crabs eating away at a man on a beach.

Sam tried not to think about that movie.

So he thought about something else. He thought about vultures. He had seen a movie once about vultures. . . .

Sam tried to switch to another channel in his mind, but, unfortunately, *Jaws* was playing.

And then there was, of course, that old science-fiction classic, *Creature from the Black Lagoon.*

Sam had seen too many movies.

He tried to make his mind a complete blank.

Tripper's voice was hoarse from calling

Sam's name. She kept listening, hoping to hear the shot that meant Sam had been found.

Tripper, Carlos, and Manuel walked up onto the grassy airfield toward the main building. They saw a ranger running toward them. He was calling Manuel.

Manuel stopped and listened to what the ranger had to say. Then he turned to Tripper and Carlos.

"He says he's getting the wisp of a radio signal on the big radio up at the office. We have quite a good antenna up there."

The ranger handed Manuel a small map. He had drawn a line on the map that went from the main building south in the direction of the Rio Claro.

"The signal is coming from that direction," Manuel said, "but, of course, it could be coming from any point along that line."

Tripper had a vivid memory of the Rio Claro from her horseback ride. The tide would be coming in now. Her head suddenly cleared.

"How could there be another radio signal?" she asked. She looked at the radio mike they had found.

"It's coming from a different direction,"

Manuel said. "It's strange. We don't use walkie-talkies anyplace on the reserve."

Suddenly Tripper turned the switch on Sam's tape recorder from Channel A to Channel B. She immediately heard sounds of breathing over the headphones and a strange muffled humming.

"I forgot!" she yelled. "There's a second radio mike. It was in his pocket."

Tripper started off at once in the direction where the signal seemed the loudest.

"Wait!" Manuel said. "It will take hours to cut through that piece of jungle. Hold still a minute, and we'll find his position by seeing where the two signals cross. We'll plot it on the map."

Tripper understood. She watched Manuel draw a second line on the map — from the place where Tripper was standing to the place where the signal was coming in the strongest. She knew that where the two lines crossed would mark the position of the second radio mike.

The lines crossed right in the middle of the Rio Claro.

"Is the tide up yet?" Tripper asked.

"No," Manuel said. "It is still a dry river-bed. We have a couple of minutes yet. And we'll get there faster if we go around by the beach and follow the Rio Claro up."

A few minutes later they saw the body wrapped in magnetic tape in the middle of the riverbed. Sam's ankles were all bloody. Food for sharks, was all Tripper could think.

But she knew he was breathing. She could hear him loud and clear over the headphones. When they went to untie him, Sam wiggled violently and shook his head back and forth. He seemed to want to tell them something very badly.

They took the gaffer tape off his mouth first — a very painful process for him.

Sam's first words were, "Don't cut the tape. The recording tape is evidence against Ted Barry."

"The tide is coming up," Manuel said. "We have to get you out of here in a hurry!"

"You're telling me!" Sam said. "Salt water would absolutely *ruin* the recording."

Manuel fired a single shot into the air.

Predawn Raid

An hour later Tripper and Sam were sitting on the porch winding the magnetic tape onto a reel. Sam's ankles were bandaged and he was missing some of his curls. They had to be cut to get the gaffer tape off his head. Other than that, he was in good shape.

"Tell me something," Tripper said. "What were you humming? I kept hearing this weird humming over the headphones."

"Soap commercials," Sam said, "tv soap commercials. It was the only way I could stop myself from thinking about scenes from horror movies."

After the tape was wound up, Manuel played it over the radio to the Park Service in San José. An hour later a message came back: The search planes had located the prospector. Rangers from the Madrigal

Station on the reserve had picked him up. The charge against him: attempted murder. There was another message. The baby parrots had been saved and were on their way back. There was no mention of either Ted Barry or Alonso.

Later that afternoon another message came over the radio. It was an encoded message. Manuel deciphered it and called Tripper and Sam into his office.

"It's for you two," Manuel said. "It's from United States Fish and Wildlife in Miami."

The message was a set of instructions. For the next seventy-two hours Tripper and Sam were not to say a word to anyone about what had happened. They were not to mention either Alonso or Ted Barry.

A secret operation was under way.

Tripper and Sam sat by the pool of the Hotel Los Portales eating lunch. They had flown back from the jungle early that morning with Dr. Vasquez and Carlos. Roger Tripper and the rest of the film crew had been very happy to see them.

The convention on wildlife was over. It had been very successful. Five new countries had agreed to sign the CITES treaty, which is an international agreement to stop the trade in endangered species. The United States and Costa Rica had signed that treaty many years before.

Sam picked a jalapeño off Tripper's plate. Sam liked hot peppers; he claimed there was no pepper too hot for him. But the next minute he was drinking down his entire glass of fruit punch.

"Wow!" Sam said. "That was the hottest pepper I've ever eaten." He looked at Tripper. "There. I saved your life. I rescued you from the pepper."

Tripper sighed. "C'mon, Sam," she said. "You've saved my life enough in my life. I only got to rescue you once."

Sam pointed to the volcano in the distance.

"*That*," he told Tripper, "is an active volcano. It might erupt any day now." He leaned back in the lounge chair and pulled his sunglasses over his eyes. "There," he said. "I did it again."

"Did what?" Tripper asked.

"Saved your life," Sam said. "I saved you from the volcano. I pointed it out to you."

Tripper laughed.

The film crew was packing up. One by

one they joined Tripper and Sam at the pool for lunch.

Tripper's father was on the phone to New York. When he joined them, he was very pleased.

"Eva says the jungle footage is terrific," he told them. The footage had been flown to the film editor in New York.

"She hasn't even seen the jaguar footage yet," Carlos said.

Coco finished putting the heavy lights away and came to sit by the pool. She stretched out in a lounge chair.

"We have to go shopping this afternoon," she said to Tripper. "It's our last day. I'll never forgive you for shopping without me."

"It was just for mosquito netting and these boots." Tripper was still wearing her boots. She had gotten used to them.

"Those boots," Coco said, "happen to be the latest thing. Everyone in Paris is wearing them."

Luis appeared at their table. "Someone is here to see you."

Right behind him was a man in a dark blue windbreaker and running shoes. His face was flushed. He was out of breath.

"Rocky Baker," he said as he shook

everyone's hand. "United States Fish and Wildlife — Miami."

He sat on a chair and grinned at Tripper and Sam. "Well," he said. "It's over. It was a success. I wanted you two to be the first to know."

Everyone listened as the agent from United States Fish and Wildlife described the events of that morning.

An hour before dawn, agents from United States Fish and Wildlife, United States Customs, and the Costa Rican Ministry of Agriculture (MAG) had raided Ted Barry's house in the suburbs of San José. They found forty parrots, fifteen scarlet macaws, and dozens of other rare birds from all over the world.

He turned to Sam. "Thanks to that tape of yours, and to additional information provided by an informant, we were able to get a search warrant for the birds. We also got arrest warrants for Ted Barry and his butler, Ralph."

"Did you get Barry?" Sam asked.

"Yes," Rocky said. "We got both of them."

"What did Ted Barry say?" Tripper asked.

Rocky laughed. "When I rolled the gold — excuse me, I mean, when I showed him my badge, he said, 'But don't you know who I *am*?'"

"What about Alonso?" Sam asked.

Rocky did not answer the question directly. "What often happens in a case like this," he said carefully, "is that the informant will get a lighter sentence even if he has actually taken part in the crime. In this case our informant has played a major role in helping us crack a multimillion-dollar smuggling ring."

Just then Luis came over to the pool to see if anyone wanted anything to eat.

"At last we eat," Sam said. "We must all be hungry. I know *I* am hungry."

Rocky burst out laughing and Tripper and Sam knew for sure who the informer must be.

"What about the birds?" Sam asked. "The ones you found in the house. What will happen to them?"

"That's a very good question," Rocky said. "Many times birds die waiting for court cases to come up. After all, the birds are the evidence. But we just got special permission to take these birds to a reserve to try to retrain them for life in the wild. Many times smugglers have clipped the birds' wings so carelessly it may take months for the feathers to grow back. And many of the birds have simply forgotten how to fly."

Coco had only been half listening to the whole thing.

"That's a very nice jacket you're wearing," she suddenly said to Rocky.

It *was* a nice jacket. It was a dark blue windbreaker with white lettering on the back: U.S. FISH AND WILDLIFE.

"We call it our raid jacket," Rocky said.

"Oh," Coco said. "And what did everybody else wear?"

Rocky was surprised. "You want to know what the Customs agents wore on the raid? And the inspectors from MAG?"

Coco nodded. "I want to know what *everyone* wore," she said happily.

Boots for Sam

After Rocky had gone, Coco said to Tripper, "Now we go shopping."

"Maybe I'll go, too," Sam said. "I might
as well get a new pair of boots while we're
down here."

"What a good idea," Tripper said
sweetly.

Sam sat in the front seat of the taxi as
they drove into San José. Tripper and Coco
sat in the back. Tripper leaned over and
whispered to Coco, "Can I use some of your
makeup?" Coco nodded and handed Tripper her mirror and her makeup case.
Tripper put her hair up in a bun.

Sam was looking out the window of the
taxi. "Hey!" he said, "did you see that? We
just passed a glass building with penguin
statues inside."

"They're made of ice," Coco said. "It's

a refrigerated playground. The children down here never get to see snow."

Suddenly Sam said, "Hey, Tripper. You look different — older or something."

"Oh, do I?" Tripper asked.

When they arrived at the shoe store Coco told the salesman she simply had to have a pair of boots with square toes just like Tripper's. . . .

". . . but for evening wear."

He was the same salesman who had waited on Tripper and Sam when they were there before.

"Evening wear?" he asked Coco.

"Yes," Coco said. "I want to wear them with my desert pants. They're made of this billowy tan chiffon and I like to wear them with this enormous tan belt."

It was always interesting to shop with Coco.

The salesman turned to Tripper and Sam. He recognized them and smiled. "Oh, I see you are back. I hope the boots were all right."

Tripper looked surprised. "Oh, you must be talking about my little sister."

"Ah," the salesman said. "There is a

strong family resemblance. What can I do for you?"

"We are looking for boots for my little brother," Tripper told him. "Sammy went and lost his best boots. Wasn't that careless?"

The salesman looked at Sam. Sam *did* look younger than Tripper just then. He had a surprised look on his face.

"I remember the boots," the salesman said. "They were good boots. What a pity."

Sam was now glaring at Tripper. He had finally caught on. But he gritted his teeth and began trying on the boots the salesman brought him.

Tripper kept up a steady stream of chatter.

"Now, Sammy," she said, "are the toes pinching? Tell the nice salesman if the toes are pinching. We don't want to get them home and *then* find out they are too small. . . . Don't growl, Sammy. Growling is bad manners. . . ."

"I'll get you for this, Tripper," Sam muttered.

"I'm not finished yet," Tripper whispered back.

"What did he say?" the salesman asked. "Do they pinch his toes?"

"Oh no," Tripper said. "The boots are fine. My little brother just wants to know if he will be getting a balloon. He always gets a balloon at our little shoe store in New York. . . ."

"Just wait, Tripper," Sam said.

SAM: ENDANGERED SPECIES!

Tripper is the beautiful daughter of a famous documentary filmmaker. Her best friend Sam, already an accomplished sound man, often works with her father. Together they are on location in Central America shooting a wildlife film in the jungle.

Tripper and Sam are suspicious of the film's sponsor, the smooth, ultraconfident Ted Barry. Why is he so reluctant to leave the film crew on their own? Who is the mysterious red-bearded man Tripper sees with him? And why does Ted Barry deny even knowing him?

When Sam mysteriously disappears, Tripper is more frightened than ever — especially when the red-bearded man is seen carrying a Could his target be Sam? Tripper has to out — before it's too late!*

33594

SCHOLA

ISBN 0-590-33594-4   RL5   011-

0 78073 00250 4

P8-CTD-822

NdZI